First paperback edition August 2021

Published by Chloe Kent August 2021
Editors & Proofread by Fiona Watson

BOOK 1 – THE SUBURBS

Book 2 – The Suburbs: Caribbean Chaos

ACKNOWLEDGMENTS

This thank you goes to the wonderful readers who have messaged me eagerly for this next instalment. Your enthusiasm has given me the little push and encouragement to do what I love.

As always, Amazon reviews are real help for an indie author, we rely heavily on your feedback.

If you have a moment spare, please leave me a little review!

Thank you again and happy reading!

Chloe xx

CHAPTER ONE

Everything, I had thought, was going to be okay.

There was no way I was going to sit there and crumble in front of Elle. I wasn't going to allow her a single ounce of smugness when she dropped that bombshell.

When I said I wasn't going anywhere, I meant it. But then again, I had no idea what Elle was about to announce next. That evening plays on my mind a lot more than it should. Each time I think about it, I grow more anxious about the whole situation.

"Remember Patrick?" Elle had called after me as Jacob and I had left the table to head back to my house.

Of course I remembered him – Patrick was the absolute creep who had tried feeling me up against his car and wouldn't take no for an answer. The type of man who has no respect for women whatsoever.

I remember how those words left her mouth, how Jacob tensed up beside me, how his hand gripped mine a little tighter and the atmosphere between us took yet another shift.

"I trust he told you about the woman that he raped?" she continued, uncomfortably imperturbable. "I'll let Jacob explain why he isn't behind bars."

I shudder as I recall those words. It doesn't matter how many times I have replayed it, her words still hit me like knives.

I guess none of what Jacob is involved with had felt real until a specific example was mentioned. Patrick really is a vile perverted man who, if dangerous, should absolutely be locked away. The fact that Jacob has had a part to play in why he isn't scares me. And makes no sense. I have seen first-hand how protective Jacob has been when these low lives have crossed the line with me. I have seen how he doesn't restrain himself from lashing out at them like they deserve – he certainly isn't helping them then. So how?

I wish I knew those answers. I wish it was just Elle lashing out and being a bitch because she wants to hurt Jacob. I wish it was a mistake and it wasn't Jacob at all. But I won't know. Not until I see him and that's going to be a little while yet.

That night, I left Jacob and Elle in their house and returned to mine. I felt like I was caught in the middle and Elle was just using me as a pawn to get to Jacob. I had to take myself out of the situation. Their marriage was ending and the very least I could do was leave them to talk it through – Elle didn't need an audience. As much as I think she thrives on it, it just didn't feel like my place to be there and witness it.

But shortly after I got home I got a phone call from a doctor in the Bahamas. My mum had collapsed during a performance on the cruise ship and been rushed to the closest hospital. At first, I wasn't sure what the panic was about. My mum has suffered from low blood pressure throughout her life and collapsing wasn't too unusual for her. Until, that is, he informed me that they couldn't wake her up. I dropped the phone, threw stuff into a carry-on bag and headed straight for the airport.

It was a bit of a blur really – I think panic just took over. I didn't even have time to search online for a flight. I just turned up and hoped that there would be at least one seat left that day. As luck would have it, I had less than three hours to wait until I was boarding the nine-hour British Airways flight to Nassau, Bahamas.

I thought a lot about sending Jacob a text message in those few hours, but I didn't want to interrupt him. His hands were full dealing with Elle and, to be honest, in that moment, I didn't feel strong enough to handle both dramas. My mum needed me and that's what I had to try and concentrate on.

The nine-hour flight passed extremely slowly. I tried to distract myself with an episode of *The Big Bang Theory*, but I soon realised I had watched the same episode three times in a row. I just couldn't escape from the chaos of my mind.

I hadn't spoken to my mum since she had told me about the affair she had behind my dad's back before I was born. I had hung up the phone and hadn't contacted her again. I vowed that as soon as I saw her, I'd tell her that I understand. I may not like it, but I understand.

I soon gave up watching any of the entertainment on offer and instead I just watched the little map showing us slowly reaching our destination. A packet of pretzels and a white wine later and we finally began our descent. It was a relief when the plane's wheels bounced gently as we landed on the tarmac. I finally knew I was close to Mum and would be with her in less than an hour. Thankfully, having no checked-in luggage meant I could get through the airport pretty quickly – there was a small queue going through arrivals, but I was soon out and into the humid air.

Getting a taxi to take me to the hospital was no problem at all. I found myself feeling a lot calmer now I was on the final leg of the journey. I laid my head back onto the seat rest and enjoyed the feeling of the air-conditioning cooling my skin. It was a hot and stuffy airport to say the least and it hadn't helped that I had been practically running to get out of there as quickly as possible. But in the car, I relaxed a little, knowing that I'd soon be with Mum.

I could see why she loves the Caribbean so much. I was absolutely in awe of the stunning tall palm trees dotted along the roadside – it made it a lot more picturesque than a British motorway, that's for sure. Everything seemed to have an extra splash of colour too – as we drove into a town, I saw locals wearing bright clothing, even random little market stalls were painted in bright blues and yellows.

I had half expected the hospital to be different, but as we pulled up it had very much the same vibe – painted in a sunshine yellow, with the car park surrounded by tall palm trees, it looked more like a posh hotel than a hospital. I couldn't wait to be able to show Mum. I could just see us, having a catch up on the beach, pina colada in hand, with her laughing that I flew all the way out here for nothing. But it wouldn't be a waste because we'd have the best few days together – I may even tell her everything about Jacob. She'll appreciate my honesty, given the fact that I have made her feel so bad about her truth.

Yes, I had thought, we'll talk, we'll laugh, we'll drink and when I know she is fully better, I'll catch a flight home, refreshed and ready to start my new chapter with my new boyfriend.

I paid my taxi fare and gathered my belongings, then enjoyed the short stroll from the car park to the entrance with the sun beating down onto my skin. The gorgeous blue skies gave me a real sense of calm. Just what I needed after the chaos of home. I had already removed my cardigan and tied my hair back off my shoulders. It was humid, in a way that made me wish I could jump into the nearest swimming pool, but first, I had to get Mum and then we could enjoy this beautiful island together. I was assuming by now that I was going to head inside the hospital and see her sitting up in bed with a silly reason as to what had caused her to collapse.

CHAPTER TWO

The hospital is quite small and seems so much quieter than our local hospital back home. The calmness is very welcoming – I usually feel quite uneasy in hospitals, especially in the emergency department. I remember my dad taking me into one many years ago when I hurt my ankle one sports day. In the first ten minutes, one woman had been constantly vomiting next to me and a man had arrived with blood gushing from his head. Between the two of them, I quickly became a shade of green myself. This hospital seemed far less daunting.

I wait for several minutes for somebody to appear at the reception desk before giving up and heading off in search of a bathroom instead. I could do with a quick freshen up after the long journey.

Thankfully, I find one quite easily and decide this is a good time to get changed. I feel a lot cooler once I'm out of my tight jeans and I manage to find a nice knee-length floaty dress in my bag. I opt for that and then give my teeth a brush and wash my face as I prepare to see Mum.

When I return to the reception desk I'm greeted by a beautiful woman with long dark braided hair and a huge friendly smile. I instantly take a liking to her. She has a very kind face.

"Hi!" she says kindly, her voice matching her smile. "Can I help you at all?"

"Yes, please," I answer with a smile, appreciating her friendliness.
"I'm looking for my mum, I got a call about her yesterday saying she collapsed."

"Oh! Mia? Wow, you were very quick. You managed to get a flight easily enough then?"

"Yes, I did. Thankfully I managed to get on one within a few hours."

"Oh, that's brilliant. Is this your first time to the Bahamas?"

"It is," I politely nod.

"How are you finding it here, so far?"

"It's such a beautiful place," I reply honestly. Suddenly, a memory of me tipsy in that Cuban bar comes into my mind. The night I thought Jacob was whisking Elle away to the Bahamas, or the *fucking Bahamas* as I referred to it. My childishness makes me smirk and I try to hold back a giggle; but the memory also makes me suddenly feel worlds apart from Jacob right now.

"Oh, great! I'm so glad to hear that. I'll find out about your mum now and if it's okay, I'll come back and get you," she says kindly before disappearing down a different hallway.

I pace quite impatiently in the waiting area. Now that I'm finally within a few metres of Mum, I suddenly realise how much I have missed her.

It slowly beings to dawn on me that I have made no arrangements for a place to stay. Maybe the hospital will let me use their Wi-Fi and I can try and find a hotel within my budget.

A couple of nurses and doctors walk by, but still no sign of the friendly receptionist. I'm growing anxious waiting around. I'm not entirely sure what is taking so long.

I get myself a Diet Coke from the vending machine and keep pacing the waiting area. My legs are too restless to sit down after the flight.

"Ah, Mia. I'm so sorry I took so long," I hear her say as she reappears, much to my relief.

"That's okay," I mumble nervously.

"So, your mum is actually having some tests right now and they're quite intricate so they can take a couple of hours. I spoke with the doctor on duty and the main doctor who has been taking care of your mum isn't working today. He's here tomorrow though and he really wants to have a conversation with you before you see your mum," she informs me.

"Okay? I'm a little confused though. Is something serious happening to my mum?"

"I'm afraid what I know is very limited," she says as she takes a step towards me. I can tell that she wants to offer me comfort, but is unsure whether she should.

"So, when should I come back?"

"The morning will be fine; I'll be here, and I can take you to your mum's doctor. He'll be able to explain everything. Is there anything else I can do for you now though?" she offers.

I pause momentarily to take in everything she has told me. I start to realise that I may have misunderstood the seriousness of my mum collapsing. This has never happened before. In the past, if it's been to do with low blood pressure, they usually keep her in for a day or two just to make sure she didn't hit her head or something. But nothing like this.

"I, um, I have nowhere to stay," I mutter. "Do you know of anywhere nearby?"

"Absolutely! There are some fabulous hotels on the island. I'll get a list for you," she says as her bright smile returns. I think she feels she can be helpful again now which seems to make her happy.

Very quickly, she taps away on her computer and brings up some glamorous-looking hotels.

"This one is just around the corner and it's breath-taking – it has four swimming pools, a private beach area for each guest and I hear the food is superb." She continues to proudly describe the hotel's amenities, but I notice the cost which instantly rules that one out.

"Actually, my budget is a lot tighter than that. Is there anything else?"

"Oh," she mumbles a little awkwardly. "The thing is, because the island is very touristy and you have arrived during a period that is very popular with the Americans, it will be hard to find something much cheaper."

Oh crap. I put a fair amount onto my credit card when I was moving, and I definitely don't have enough funds to cover more than just a few days at one of these hotels.

"Um… okay. Are there any hostels?"

"Hostels here are more for the homeless and not for travellers," she says with an element of concern in her voice. "Leave it with me, I'll see what I can sort out. Grab a seat and I'll make some calls."

I smile gratefully and reluctantly sit down to wait.

Suddenly, I feel like everything is hitting me like one huge wave. My mum is seriously ill, and I'm running so low on funds that I'm worried I'll barely have enough money to feed myself out here, let alone pay these hotel prices. But I can't just fly home, my mum needs me.

On top of that, I haven't spoken to Jacob yet, and I have no idea what is happening back home with him and Elle. I don't know if he is okay. This is probably the most out of control I have ever felt in my life and I'm not sure if I am built for it.

I see the receptionist chatting away intently on the phone. I realise I haven't gotten her name yet and I should, considering how helpful she has been.

Eventually, she nods and smiles before hanging up the phone and turning to me.

"Good news, I managed to find a room in a local B&B. It's only a ten-minute walk away. It's not the most upmarket of places, but she said she can do it for twenty dollars a night, if that helps you."

My face instantly lights up at her words.

"Yes! Thank you so, so much," I say with a sigh of relief.

"You're welcome. I'm sorry it can't be anything much better."

"It's fine, really. As long as I can get some sleep and be here for my mum, I'm happy. You've been so kind and more than helpful and yet I didn't even catch your name."

She smiles pleasantly. "I'm Drea."

"Thank you again, Drea. I'll see you tomorrow morning," I say before grabbing my bags.

"You sure will! Here's the address of the B&B, but it should be quite easy to find. Just keep walking until you get to the top of the hill and you should see it. It has a bright yellow door."

I smile gratefully before heading out through the entrance doors and back into the hot and humid air.

CHAPTER THREE

These ten minutes feel like the longest in my life. The heat hits differently when you're dragging a heavy bag up a steep hill. The adrenaline has kept me wide awake this entire time, but now, the tiredness is really starting to kick in. It's almost three in the afternoon here, which means it's almost eight in the evening back home. Definitely a long time to be awake. I feel quite anxious to get to the hotel and get my phone switched back on and charged up so I can give Jacob a call; he must be wondering where I have gotten to by now, especially if he has gone to my house to see me and realised I am not there.

I'm relieved when I see a sign for Ocean West, which is the road name for the B&B. Soon, I spot the bright yellow wooden door, just like Drea described. From a distance, it looks okay, but the closer I get, the more I realise the area is a little intimidating.

The building itself looks quite worn and the street it's on is quite dirty. Rubbish is scattered around the building and most of the nearby shops either look equally worn or are simply closed down and abandoned.

An elderly skinny man sits smoking just outside the entrance of the B&B; he stares at me curiously the closer I get. I don't feel threatened by him in the slightest, he just seems intrigued as to why I am here. I think maybe I look quite out of place. I can't imagine this area sees many tourists.

"Mia?" a small elderly lady surprises me by saying as the yellow door swings open.

"Yes?"

"Oh good. Drea said you wouldn't be long. Please, come in," she says as she gestures me inside the dark hallway.

It's amazing and unsettling how dark the room becomes the second she closes the door behind us. Almost as if it isn't daylight at all.

It's small inside and not particularly inviting. There is a tiny reception area which reminds me of a very olde-worlde pub back home, it has that old-fashioned dark wood which just looks a bit tired. There aren't many windows in reception, which probably explains the weird musty smell. I don't think this place gets much fresh air.

Nonetheless, I'm grateful. It means I can be here with my mum and it's only twenty dollars a night, which means I can afford to be here for at least a few weeks, which will hopefully be enough time to support her.

"Here are your keys. I need paying daily. If I'm not here, just leave the money at reception. Oh, and I lock the main door at eleven at night," she informs me as she begins to lead the way to my room.

She has a much thicker accent than Drea did, so it's quite hard to catch what she says each time because she speaks much faster, but I kind of love that authenticity about her.

Whilst I am grateful, I almost want to cry when I see my room – it's tiny. So tiny in fact that I can't help but wonder whether Harry Potter had more space under his stairs than I do now.

There is one tiny square window with bars over it that can't be opened. In the corner of the room is a single camp bed with a thin mattress on top and no bed sheets. The bathroom area is like a small wet room – just a very old-looking shower head right next to the toilet, surrounded by small tiles that you can tell used to be white, but are now a yellowish brown.

"You can buy bedding from a shop a few blocks away or the market. We used to serve breakfast, but I had to stop doing that a few years ago because I'm getting too old. So, you'll have to feed yourself." She speaks very bluntly, but there's no intended rudeness behind her tone. She just strikes me as a very straight-to-the point woman.

By the time I put my bags down, the elderly lady is already closing my door behind her as she leaves. The closing of the door makes my room feel darker, smaller and even lonelier.

It's one of those places where you aren't sure if you even want to sit down. I feel like some creepy crawlies are probably lurking under the bed or in the cracks of the walls.

Sure enough, just as the thought comes to my mind, my theory is proven true when a large brown bug randomly appears from behind the bed and crawls up the wall. It looks like a cockroach, but I try not to focus on it too much because the thought is already making me shudder.

I dive straight into my bag and pull out a charger and adapter for my phone. There is only one plug socket in the corner of the room, but I don't care. It'll do.

I then drink the rest of my Diet Coke, which unfortunately has gotten warm in the sun, but it's all I have and I'm too tired to go venturing back out for another drink.

I pull out a beach towel from my bag and place it on top of the bed and perch on the end. The bug has crawled over to the other wall, but I keep half an eye on it in the hope that it doesn't wander back over.

Out of nowhere, I think about Puss and suddenly and forcefully I'm bursting into tears. I wonder where she is and if she is okay. The thought of her lost in some woods, completely alone, scared, confused and abandoned because of that cold bitch makes my heart ache.

Funny how my mum is seriously ill, I miss Jacob, I'm stuck in this hell hole and the thing that tips me over the edge is Puss. Maybe the reality is that I was already so close to the edge.

I fight the negative thoughts that are making me sob and tell myself that I can't wallow now. I have to stay strong. I have my mum to think about.

My phone seems to be taking forever to turn back on; I didn't even realise my battery had drained.

I feel so tired now that it's a struggle just to hold my head up. I cautiously lie down on the bed, praying that no more creepy crawlies are about to appear. I stay on my side with my knees tucked up to my chest as high as they can be. Somehow, this makes me feel slightly safer.

I rest my heavy eyes, just for a minute I think, just until my phone comes back on, although, even as I think this, I can already feel myself relaxing and drifting off into a deep sleep.

CHAPTER FOUR

I'm awoken by the sound of my phone vibrating against the small wooden bedside table and the bright flashing from my screen. Instantly, I grab it, already knowing who it will be.

"Hello?" I croak. My throat is dry, I'm so thirsty, but I do my best to sit up straight and compose myself.

"Mia? Where are you? What's happening? I've been knocking at your door for ages," Jacob says in a rush, with a slight tone of panic.

"Don't worry, I can explain."

"We are okay, aren't we? You're not having second thoughts?"

"No," I answer simply, a small smile appearing on my lips. His need to have reassurance from me is adorable and I love it.

"Okay, okay, good," he says and his voice calms down a little to a more relaxed tone.

"Can you let me in then? I thought we could talk."

"Oh, I can't. I'm not there, I'm in the Bahamas."

"The *Bahamas!?*" Jacob questions, his voice getting anxious again.

"It's Mum..." I begin and the reality of telling somebody else about it makes my emotions rush to the surface and I have to fight back the tears just to get my words out.

"Take your time…" he whispers into the handset, almost like he can see that I'm about to cry.

"I'm scared Jacob. I don't think she's going to be okay."

"Oh, Mia. Fuck." He sighs deeply and I can really feel how sad he is for me. I can hear his shoes against the wooden floor back in his kitchen and I know he is pacing anxiously.

"I'm so sorry. What happened?"

"I don't really know yet. I just got this phone call to say she had collapsed, and they haven't been able to wake her since. I have a meeting with the doctor who has been taking care of her tomorrow. Hopefully I'll understand more then."

"Fuck. Baby. I'm so sorry. What time is it there?" he asks gently, his voice delicate and compassionate.

"It's nearly five in the morning. You?"

"Shit. It's almost ten in the morning here. I'm so sorry for waking you up baby. Go back to sleep."

"It's okay. I'm awake now," I say, as I see a slight sunrise out of the barred window.

"So, Ellc has only just left then?"

"Yeah. It was a fucking long night." He groans, sounding exhausted.

"Is everything okay?" I ask nervously but I need to know.

"I think so. But honestly, I couldn't give a fuck about any of it right now. It's you I'm worried about. Are you in Nassau? I'll get a flight out."

"I am yes, but you don't need to do that. You have work and I won't be much company anyway."

"Company? Mia I'm not flying out and expecting you to sip sangria on the beach and rub sunblock into my back. I want to fly out to be there for you. I want to support you through this," he says, sounding slightly offended that I'm brushing him off.

I need him more than anything right now. But I just know that when he is here, I'll start questioning him about the things that Elle said, and I'm worried I won't like what he has to say about it; and I can't afford to use up my energy on that situation.

"Jacob, I am all my mum has, you know?" I say softly. "I love you, but I need to concentrate on her right now. I just don't have any head space left to worry about what Elle was saying."

"But Mia, none of what Elle said is quite what you think. Well, some of it is; and I'm not proud of a lot of it, but I know you'll understand. It's not quite as terrible as she wants you to believe," he says so desperately that I feel a sting as my eyes water. I press the phone tightly against my ear as if it's somehow bringing me closer to him.

"I hope not," I mumble as I fight back yet more tears and let out a false and awkward laugh.

"Mia?"

"It's fine Jacob, honestly. We'll talk about it when I'm back. I just need to concentrate on one thing at a time."

"I understand," he says unconvincingly. "Have you sorted somewhere to stay?"

I look around the old stale room, with no fresh air and barely any light, and I almost tell him the truth. That I am in some depressing dirty room that is a replica of a dodgy prison cell and that I hate it.

But I swallow my pride.

"Yeah, I'm sorted in a little bed and breakfast around the corner from the hospital where my mum is. I'm fine," I lie, but hopefully convincing him.

I don't want to be like Elle and have Jacob spend his money on me. I know as soon as I tell him the truth, he'll have me in some over-priced hotel within the hour and I don't want to be that person. Jacob liked the fact I was independent and that I had my own career and my own money. I don't ever want to morph into some kind of desperate housewife.

"Okay, well I'm pleased you got somewhere sorted so quick. Have you eaten?"

"I had some pretzels on the plane if what's what you mean?" I say and giggle at his fussing, but from his tone I can tell he isn't in much of a jokey mood. "I'm fine, honestly, please don't worry about me. I'll check in with you later okay?"

There's a short pause before Jacob mumbles something about keeping him updated, which I promise to do. I assure him again that I'll be fine before I end the call. I can tell he didn't want to get off the phone, nor is he impressed that I haven't asked him to jump on a plane to join me. But hopefully, he understands and isn't offended. I love Jacob, I think we will be okay, I just need to be here first. I can't be distracted.

CHAPTER FIVE

I haven't woken up anywhere near as refreshed as I hoped. My neck and all around the back of my head is heavily aching from trying to sleep on that tiny pillow and thin mattress. My skin feels horribly dry from the long-haul flight and I'm so thirsty I could drink water out of a drainpipe.

But the sun is shining on this beautiful island and today I will get to see my mum. The anticipation of knowing she is here has made me feel ridiculously excited to see her again. It's rare that I'm even in the same country as my mum and now that I finally am, I just want to be with her. It's strange, I love my mum, but I don't usually feel this way. Not since I was a child anyway.

It reminds me of a time when I was in primary school, I must have only been five or six years old, and I remember my dad happily telling me that Mum was returning from the cruise ship for a couple of months and she'd be there at the school gates that afternoon to pick me up.

I was so excited! I asked my dad to put my hair in two plaits that morning just for her – it wasn't my favourite hairstyle, but I knew how much my mum loved plaits on me. I then told everyone who would listen that my mum was coming to collect me that afternoon. I remember sitting in class and gazing out of the window to the school gates and eagerly waiting for that final school bell to ring. And when that moment finally came, it didn't disappoint.

My cool mum was standing at the gate, waving energetically, her thick brunette hair in a stylish bob, black sunglasses on, beautifully bronzed skin and the brightest smile. She looked like a famous person. Totally glamorous and chic. I ran across that playground so fast I thought my legs were going to buckle beneath me. Thankfully, they didn't. I threw myself into my mum's arms and for some reason, the second my cheek pressed against her shoulder as she embraced me, I burst into tears. I couldn't understand why at the time – I was so happy, so why was I crying?

Now I know that tears can come when we are happy too and I really was, it was overwhelming, it was exciting, it was brilliant. After seven long months at sea, my mum was back.

Sometimes you don't realise how much you have missed a person until they're stood right in front of you.

I'm wearing a light-yellow midi dress, very airy and cool. Yellow is my mum's favourite colour, so it had to be this dress today. My hair is pulled up into a messy bun and I throw on some flip flops before heading out of the door.

The sun causes me to squint quite a lot – I had forgotten how dark and dull it was in the B&B until I was back outside again, under the aqua blue skies.

Halfway down the hill is a tiny little café; it looks old and a bit worn out but somehow, this just adds to its character. It is painted pale blue and white and really reminds me of a little seaside café I used to go to with my dad after we dropped Mum back off at the port to begin her next several months at sea. My dad always knew that I took it hard and he would take me to the café without fail after we said our goodbyes and treat me to a banana split and a cream soda.

I don't really believe in fate or anything like that, but right now I can't help but wonder whether I was always supposed to find this little café, so that I could be reminded of Dad. It's almost as if he is right here with me, watching over me – he must know that I need him right now. It's comforting.

I pop inside to gather some drinks and snacks to keep me going for the morning, I order two bottles of water to keep in my bag because I definitely need to rehydrate today. I order a strong coffee as well to hopefully perk me up after an uncomfortable night's sleep and lastly, I order a cinnamon bun, for no other reason than the fact sugar and pastry would go down a treat right now.

By the time I reach the bottom of the hill with my coffee in my hand, my legs have gone a little like jelly. I'm suddenly nervous. If I'm honest I have been quite nervous all night about speaking with Mum's doctor, but now that I'm here, I can't just try and ignore it any longer.

I'm a little gutted when I'm not greeted by Drea's bright smile; instead an older man, possibly in his sixties, greets me. He seems friendly enough, but I somehow needed the kindness and familiarity of Drea this morning.

"Hi, I'm Mia, I'm supposed to be meeting with…"

"Yes, yes, come with me," the man interrupts, already leading the way down the hallway.

All the typical hospital smells and noises take over and there's definitely no escaping where I am now, and I hate it. But I'm here for Mum, and I'm going to stay strong.

"In here." The man points as he ushers me inside a small but well-decorated office. "I'll tell Dr Garcia that you are here."

"Thank you," I mumble and awkwardly take my seat in front of the formal brown desk.

I try to take my mind away from the anxiety I feel waiting here to finally get some understanding of what has happened to my mum. I'm distracted quite easily by a map of the world. I quickly find the Bahamas, and notice how close it is to the United States, well Florida at least. Then my eyes scan across the map and land on England. I glance back at where I am and then again back at

England, where Jacob is, and my stomach feels knotted. It surprises me how much I miss him.

I wonder what he is up to, what he might be wearing, how his hair might be styled today. I think about his broad shoulders and the safety they bring me when I'm cuddled into them. I think about how he protected me against Alex, how he kissed every bruise and graze until I relaxed enough to drift off to sleep that horrible night after the attack. I think back to how he makes me feel when I'm with him. It's hard to describe, but the only word I can land on inside my head is *seen*. Jacob makes me feel seen. For everything I am and for everything I want to be. He sees me.

"Ah, Ms Johnson." A deep voice startles me out of my thoughts.

I turn to finally meet my mum's doctor. He is tall and dark with a typical pearly white American smile. His instant friendliness reminds me of how sweet Drea was when I first arrived. That instantly makes me feel relieved.

"Hello," I croak a little nervously, but offer up a smile in return.

"Can I get you a drink or anything?"

"Thank you, but I'm okay, I got a coffee on the way in."

"Oh, awesome, okay. I'm sorry I wasn't here for you yesterday; I didn't realise you would be here so soon, and I was doing some work at a nearby clinic," he explains, apologetically.

"Ah, that's really okay. I didn't expect to get here so quickly either, plus I needed the sleep anyway!" I try to joke to ease my nerves.

"Oh, good. I'm glad you got some rest. Is anyone else joining us? I wasn't sure if you had siblings coming too?"

"Erm, no," I answer, taken aback by the question. But then suddenly it dawns on me why he has asked it. He thinks I'm going to need support, that's why he is asking if there is anyone else. "It's just me."

"Ah, I see. Well there is quite a lot to go through. A lot of medical jargon but if you don't understand anything, just ask and I'll explain…"

"I just need to know first, Dr Garcia, what is it I can expect?"

He sighs sympathetically as he scans over his notes and then looks up straight into my eyes.

"It's not good news, Mia."

CHAPTER SIX

I pause for what feels like an awkwardly long time, but I just want to compose myself long enough to sit through this meeting without crying in front of a total stranger.

"Then please, Dr Garcia, if it's not good news, can you spare me the long report and medical jargon? And just tell me straight what has happened?" I say so emotionally that it's a strain to get my words out without my throat hurting. I hate that feeling when you get a lump in your throat before the tears come. Holding them back only makes it hurt more.

He nods understandingly and leans closer to me, as if he is sharing a secret.

"From what we can gather, your mum had an accident on the ship where a light fixture fell from the ceiling and hit her on the side of her head. Apparently, she was knocked out but came around quite quickly and felt well enough not to seek any medical help," he begins and I slowly nod.

"However, within a couple of days she was complaining to staff of having headaches and vision issues before collapsing. I'm so sorry Mia, but your mum has had a very serious bleed on the brain."

"Can't that be fixed?" I interrupt in disbelief. I'm no expert but they work miracles on *Grey's Anatomy.* And just like in the show,

I want him to tell me that there's a chance they can still fix this. No matter how small the chance might be. Then by some dramatic turn of events he manages to save my mother's life and we all have a happy ending here.

"If a patient comes to us within twenty-four hours there's usually around a sixty percent chance that we can stop the bleed and any swelling and we'd expect them to make a recovery. However, by day two, this greatly decreases to just twenty percent. Unfortunately your mum got to us on day three," he explains softly.

"I still don't understand," I sigh in frustration. "I'm sorry, I don't mean to be rude, but I just don't understand. What percent chance of survival are we on now?"

"That's the thing, as doctors we weren't sure how much hope we could expect.
Patients don't usually make day three. Your mum is strong but I'm afraid to say that we quickly concluded that if she were to ever wake up, she would have severe brain damage."

I go to speak but my jaw feels locked. I can't say a word, barely even a sound. I just sit staring at Dr Garcia, or rather, through him.

"This is why we needed to speak with you first. You need to understand what to expect. Your mum cannot breathe anymore without her life support. It is a very daunting thing to witness. I wish I had better news, but you asked for the blunt truth, and the truth is, that this is the end of the road for your mother. I am so very sorry."

"I..." I go to speak again but my mouth is so dry it's just a strained whisper. My mouth always becomes dry right before a panic attack.

"We need to go through the paperwork and discuss turning off the machines and allowing her to go peacefully," he continues. And I know he is doing his job and I know I asked him to get to the point, but I think if he mentions anything more about my mum, about life support machines or her brain, I'm going to pass out.

"Stop," I whisper, whilst I put both hands on his desk and steady myself. I feel like I'm swaying. Or the room is moving. Either way, I feel like I could pass out, or have a panic attack, or both.

Without saying another word, Dr Garcia gets up and opens all the windows around me. He kneels down next to me and places a paper cup filled with cold water in my shaky hands.

"Drink this," he says gently but authoritatively.

I do as he says and the cold water instantly eases the strain on my throat a little, enough to make me feel like I can breathe easier.

"I need some time," I mumble. "Away from here."

"I understand. I'll be here until nine o'clock tonight. Why don't you come back this evening? Have some time to process all the information and we'll chat later."

I nod and carefully pull myself up to my feet. I'm wobbly and lightheaded but I can't bear to sit in this chair a moment longer.

I need to get out of here.

"Would you like me to take you to see your mum first?" he offers, just as I almost make it out of the door.

I turn and look into his eyes. I try to think of a reasonable excuse not to, but I can't think of one.

"I just can't right now," is all I manage to muster up.

He nods as if he understands and I don't need to explain why.

**

For someone who was about to pass out, I did well to make it to the beach. I didn't even plan on coming here but it is where I have ended up. I feel calmer here, like I can process my thoughts without them being too loud. If that makes any sense.

It's quiet here, it's obviously not the main beach where all the tourists congregate, but it's perfect. The ocean is turquoise, the sand is almost white, the palm trees around me are ridiculously tall – they make me feel tiny. It's the kind of picture-perfect scene you expect to see as a screen saver on an old computer. I needed this.

I look out towards the ocean and watch the waves roll in, watching how white the tips of the waves become right before they gently smother the sand. I think about how many happy years my mum spent cruising these exact oceans. This was her main route. When I was a child it was mostly cruises from Southampton which would sail around the Mediterranean, but for as long as I can remember now, she's been here, working for Royal Caribbean. They usually begin in Fort Lauderdale, Florida. She then sails from there to the Bahamas, Cuba, Haiti and usually back again but on a slightly different route stopping at different ports.

I know this and yet when she would tell me all about it, I'd pretend I was barely listening. I wish I hadn't done that. I know why I did it – I was mad. I've been a bit mad with her ever since I was a kid, and especially when Dad died. It felt like she abandoned me. It felt like for her there was nothing worth staying at home for and that always made me feel sad, like Dad and I weren't good enough for her.

She invited me on board with her so many times. She asked me to take a gap year after university and sail around the Caribbean with her. But I made my excuses not to. I felt as though, if I were to do that, then I'd be pretty much forgiving her for all those things I was mad about. Ridiculous now when I look back. I should have just gone with her. At least then perhaps I could have been honest and told her how much I missed her as a child. Instead of being a coward and avoiding the subject but subtly making her feel like I didn't care much about her. When I did care, so much.

I'm so fucking angry at myself right now. What a fuck up. Why do we do this in life? Why do we wait until it's too fucking late to have some kind of realisation or epiphany? What a waste of time. And now there's nothing I can do. I can't holiday with my mum in the Bahamas like I thought I could, I can't take her up on a cruising trip, I can't tell her how much I love her. She's gone. She's physically here, but her mind is gone and that's it. Time's up. Game over.

I waited too fucking long and now look.

I pull my phone out of my bag and quickly find Jacob's number.

"She's going to die," I almost yell as he answers my call.

"What?"

"She had a head injury. It caused a bleed on the brain. Now she's brain dead and I have to turn off the machines and she's going to die, and you know what else?"

"What?" he barely says before I yell over him.

"I didn't fucking cruise with her! She asked and asked again, and I said no. I said I was busy. I said I wasn't a fan of boats. I basically told her to fuck off and yet all she wanted was to spend time with me, just like I always wanted as a kid. So why did I say no?"

"I don't…"

"I'll tell you why!" I interrupt. "Because I'm fucking pathetic. Or stubborn. Or both. Now it's too fucking late. She's going to die Jacob, die. And that's it. Any chance to do anything with her is over."

"Right, Mia, where is it you're staying?" His voice is louder to speak over me.

"Oh, just some glorious shit hole where there's no water but hey, at least the bugs are free."

"Bugs?"

"Roaches actually."

"Mia, why didn't you ask for my help? I could have sorted you somewhere better to stay."

"Jacob, my mum is dying and all you're hearing are roaches? I couldn't give a shit," I snap.

"I care about where you're staying because I love you. You don't want me to fly out, so I'm limited with how I can help. But I can help with this."

I pause, listening to his words. They're kind and caring but I don't want that. I don't even feel like I deserve it; really, I just wanted to rant and argue.
And now I have run out of things I want to say.

"I'm not ready for her to go yet," I whimper, as a single tear falls down my cheek and I hang up the phone.

CHAPTER SEVEN

I sit on the beach for a further two hours before I feel like I am ready to move. My legs are like jelly when I stand up. I could have continued sitting here well into the afternoon, but I force myself to move. I need to eat. I need to walk. Anything really, but I can't just sit anymore. I'm allowing myself to become too numb and I mustn't let that happen. Mum isn't gone yet, she's still here and she still needs me to be strong enough to hold her hand until the very end.

I decide to head towards the market and look for something for Mum and for me too. Like a matching bracelet or necklace. Something we can both have. I think she would have loved that.

I'm loving all the bright vivid colours I see from the market stalls the closer I get. There's a fruit and vegetable stall which is just bursting with colour. Huge watermelons, large oranges, coconuts and brightly coloured peppers. It's literally a perfect rainbow display of healthy foods. I wish I had a cooker or something back in my room, I'd definitely whip up a nice soup or something with the vegetables from this stall.

Some of the stalls are a bit tacky which makes me smile fondly as I think about how much Mum would appreciate all the funny lighters and fridge magnets, along with the typical 'I heart Bahamas' t-shirts.

I then notice a stall with stunning ornaments and figurines

carved out of wood. Funnily enough, Mum always brought Dad one of them every time she returned home. I'm not quite sure that Dad loved them as much as Mum did, but he was always grateful. Before I left home, we must have collected around eleven or twelve of them. We had a tiger one, an elephant, one of a small boat, one of an old man sitting on a bench which, come to think of it, is actually quite random. My favourite one was a huge palm tree that Mum brought home the day she came to meet me at the school gates.

"Excuse me ma'am," a smiley young man calls from another stall. "Excuse me ma'am, but you're not smiling."

"Sorry." I shrug, awkwardly.

"It's the Bahamas, ma'am. You have to smile!" he says so cheerfully that his enthusiasm makes me giggle a bit.

As soon as I giggle, his smile grows even wider, if that's possible; he's clearly ecstatic that he got a smile out of me.

I approach his small stall which is actually just a drinks station.

"Ma'am, have you tried a Bahamian goombay punch?"

"No, never." I shake my head.

"Today you will! A gift, from us, the people of the Bahamas, to you," he offers ever so kindly.

He gathers a large cup and fills it halfway with ice cubes which immediately makes my mouth water. It looks so cold and refreshing already.

Next, he pours in a slightly slushy yellow drink and tops it with half a fresh passionfruit and a wedge of pineapple.

"Here," he says eagerly. "Try it."

I take a small sip and the sweetness instantly hits my mouth and fills my tastebuds with fruitiness.

"Wow!" I smile again, gratefully.

It's very sweet – it mostly tastes like pineapple, but it's absolutely delicious.

"You like?!"

"I do! Very much so. Thank you, thank you," I say between sips.

The man throws his arms up in the air as if he just won a challenge and I giggle again. For a few short minutes, this stranger has made me forget my problems and I couldn't appreciate it more.

I continue walking through the middle of the market under the glorious sunshine until I eventually find a little homemade jewellery shop.

There is so much to look at and to choose from that it's hard to decide. There are stunning little rings with cute turtles on them, earrings with pearls on them and little gems. So many adorable pieces. I wish Mum was here so we could choose together.

"That crystal is my favourite," a lady says as she clocks me staring at all the colourful crystals on the table.

"Oh?"

"Yes. You break it in two and you give one half to your friend or soulmate and it's supposed to draw you back together. So, no matter where you'll be in the world, one day it'll bring you back together," she passionately informs me.
I can tell she's a very smart woman and knows a lot about crystals.

"That's actually perfect," I mumble, hiding my face awkwardly in case I start to cry.

"Who is it for sweetheart?"

"My mum..."

"Ah. I see." She nods sympathetically. "And where is she?"

"She's here..." I manage to say before my throat thickens again with emotion.
"But she's in the hospital. She's not well."

I can feel the lady staring at me intently, but I try not to make eye contact. I just know I'm going to cry if she asks any more questions.

"You know, on the island we don't believe death is the end," she says and I realise how good she is at reading people. I must have it written all over my face.

I nod politely as she gently places her hand on my shoulder, as if to comfort me.

"The spirit of your mum will always be with you, she will always find you when you need her the most and one day, not too soon, you'll meet her and any loved ones you've ever lost. It's not the end, that much I know," she says quietly so that none of the other people at the stall can hear us. It's sweet and comforting and somehow, I now feel more than ever that I was supposed to find this crystal and meet this kind woman.

"Thank you," I manage to say, holding back my emotions. "You're very kind."

"Here…" she says as she takes the crystal and puts it into a little felt bag.

"Oh, I don't have much cash on me…"

"It's a gift." She smiles as she places the small bag in the palm of my hand.

I instantly know that, before I go home, I'll be sure to come and purchase some of her lovely jewellery, so that I can go some way to paying her back for her kindness.

"Are you sure? I'm not sure I can accept that. It's so kind, but I have to give you something."

She nods and holds her smile to reassure me.

I'm a little bit speechless at how friendly people are on this island. It's like everyone wants to help and support each other. You certainly wouldn't have this back in London, or even in the Suburbs.

"Say no more about it. You're very welcome…?"

"Oh! Mia!" I quickly answer to fill the blanks.

"Mia. You're very welcome, Mia." She smiles. "I'm Anita."

"Anita." I nod gratefully. "I'm very happy I got to meet you. Thank you so much for all your help. I'll take these to my mum tonight."

She nods and turns to continue putting out some of her stock like she was when I first came in.

"See you soon, Mia," she calls after me.

"See you soon." I smile before I leave.

CHAPTER EIGHT

I feel quite humbled and very comforted by the people I have met today. Everyone seems a little kinder than back home. Maybe it's the weather; I would definitely be smiling more if we had this gorgeous sun shining every day. The longer I'm here, the more I understand why my mum found it so hard to tear herself away. I can imagine it was quite freeing and exhilarating to live out of a suitcase and travel around these stunning islands – although I don't think it'll ever stop hurting that she preferred this life to the one we had at home. I was at home. What could these islands offer that we couldn't?

I'm tired now. My legs are aching, and my face feels tight and tired from the sun. I need a proper wash and, ideally, I just want to collapse onto a bed and close my eyes for ten minutes. Today has been a lot to take in and process and it's very much on my mind that it's about to get worse.

I am slowly making my way to the steep hill up to the B&B when my phone pings in my pocket. It's Jacob.

For a moment I'm a little confused at the message as it simply reads:

The Ocean Club, Four Seasons Resort.

Within seconds another message pops up on the screen.

I can't bear the thought of you going through all this and not having somewhere decent to sleep at the end of the day. Reservation's in your name. For as long as you need. P.S Try and fight your natural urges to be stubborn and just go.

I smile at the last line. He knows me well enough to know that of course I want to protest. I don't want to rely on a man, I like doing things for myself, however, this offer is too hard to pass up right now. I ache, I'm groggy, I'm emotionally run down and also, the fact that he has gone ahead and arranged this despite knowing I'd probably be a pain in the ass about it means a lot.

Knowing I have such an incredible upgrade makes me walk up that hill a lot quicker than I thought I could manage.

I'm so relieved when I make my way back into the small poky room and know that I don't have to stay here any longer. I'm so grateful that Drea found this place for me, and I'm definitely not some kind of snob who can't cope with a bit of dust and dirt, but this place really is the type of room you'd expect to see in an abduction movie where the victims are finally found hidden in some weird bloke's basement; or maybe I've just watched too many crime documentaries! Either way, I'm out of here.

I leave some cash on the side for the elderly woman and a little thank you note, and I head back out into the Bahamian sun. I head straight down to the taxi rank at the bottom of the hill and my heart starts to race in anticipation of the new hotel I'm about to go to. The thought of having a nice bubble bath and a soft bed to sit on makes me feel like it's my birthday and Christmas rolled into one.

"Hi." I smile as I head towards the first taxi I see. "Can I go to The Ocean Club Hotel please?"

"Of course, jump in," he responds cheerily. "Great choice by the way – The Ocean Club probably has the best views of the island."

I smile warmly at his information. The idea of a gorgeous, picturesque view gives me butterflies in my stomach. I'm so eager to get there – I feel as though I'll be instantly jumping on the bed with a big bag of popcorn to celebrate, just like Kevin in *Home Alone*.

The only downside that I'm noticing so far is that I'm a lot further away from the hospital than I was in the B&B, but taxis seem to be readily available and not too expensive so it's not the end of the world.

"We're almost here," the taxi driver tells me as we approach a smaller road right in front of the white sandy beach that takes us up to the beautifully immaculate hotel.

Everything is white wood and looks so clean you'd think it was brand new. I love how neatly set out it is with lots of greenery, beautiful flowers and, of course, plenty of tall palm trees. It looks like a dreamy backdrop for an advert for a Caribbean wedding.

I pay the driver and head up to reception as quickly as my tired feet will allow.

I'm met with the coolness of the air-conditioning against my skin and a complimentary glass of water with ice and lemon from an employee.

"Is it just you, Ms Johnson?" she asks, without taking her eyes off her computer screen.

I'm already sipping my refreshing water so I just nod and hope she notices.

"Fabulous. I'll get you a key and help with your, err, bags?" She stops herself, confused, as one of her dark eyebrows arches at my one lonely-looking holdall.

"Ah, don't worry. This is my only bag. I'll carry it," I offer, awkwardly.

"Do you have everything you need?" she asks quizzically, as if nobody has ever arrived at this hotel with just the one bag.

"Yeah, I'm fine." I try to answer breezily but I still feel awkward because she seems so confused.

"We have some shops in the second lobby, just in case you need anything else."

"Great, I'll keep it in mind."

There's no judgement in her tone, she still comes across as very friendly, she's just slightly confused and even concerned that I'm underprepared for my stay.

"All the refreshments in your room are complimentary and will be changed every day," she informs me as I follow her down the white-tiled hall, admiring all the plants along the way.

It has that fresh holiday smell. You know the one – the mixture of humid air, sun cream and excitement. Suddenly I have the urge to get into my hotel room as quickly as possible and smell the fresh towels and bedsheets. I'm pretty sure that's quite weird, and nobody does that, but I genuinely feel like a child again, starting my first holiday.

"Here we are." She smiles pleasantly as the dark oak door swings open, unveiling a light airy beautiful room.

My eyes flicker across each section of the room. I'm not sure what I want to focus on first. The bed? It's huge – it looks like it could comfortably fit four of me. Maybe the bathroom? The bathtub is not disappointing, it's a huge oval shape with a dozen hair products and fresh soaps for me to try. I just want to dive into it right now and load it up with sensual bath soak and a tonne of bubble bath.

The air-conditioning is on so high that the room feels wonderfully refreshing. I realise how I must look to the kind receptionist, gawking the way that I am, and I quickly close my mouth and desperately try to take a cooler, more casual approach instead.

"Is everything satisfactory?"

"Satisfactory!? It's fucking amazing," I answer, not at all cool or casual.

"Awesome." She smirks, looking as if she's trying not to laugh at my over-excitement.

"I have stayed in posh hotels before," I begin to say, not really knowing why I have to give an explanation, but I find myself doing it anyway. "Like, I'm usually much calmer than this. You know, because a hotel is a hotel and I'm obviously an adult and usually very composed. I am absolutely not going to belly flop onto that bed as soon as you close the door."

"Uh-huh." She nods, not really believing me. "I'll close the door now and let you get on with your adult stuff; please be careful not to hurt yourself when diving on the bed though, okay?"

She smiles again before closing the door behind her. I can't help but giggle as she leaves – we both know I'm about to dive onto this huge bed!

I never really knew what was meant by the term 'four-poster bed' but I guess this is it. It's like a bed you'd see a picture of in a fairy-tale book, beautifully fit for a princess. It has gorgeous white drapes around the sides, which definitely triggers my inner child – young Mia would definitely have had fun pretending she was some damsel in distress, waiting for her prince charming to save her from the fire-breathing dragon before whisking her away to a magical new kingdom.

Holy shit. The view! The white shutters have already been opened for me; they slide neatly into the wall, exposing in all its beauty the huge private veranda followed by my own section of private beach. The doors must open almost ten feet wide – it's absolutely breath-taking. It feels so open, just how I like it, just how I have my own house back home. I love natural light, openness, the feeling of freedom – and it's all here, all in this room. I feel so incredibly lucky. I truly feel like I am staring at a piece of paradise; and as much as I am so grateful, I am suddenly saddened. The thought of my mum drifts back into my mind as I think about her lying in the hospital. I wish she could see this view with me. I'd give anything for her to be in this room with me, right now, in this moment. The harsh reality forces my excitement to take a back seat as I'm met with the all too familiar rush of dread, fear and sadness.

I suddenly feel so small in this enormous room. Why did I tell Jacob not to come?

CHAPTER NINE

I didn't want to admit it, especially to Jacob, but he was right to book me something else and I appreciate it so much. This hotel room has made me feel revived again and I really needed that. I spent around an hour in the bathtub, going through almost every bottle of bath wash I could find, scrubbing away the last forty-eight hours as best I could. Of course, you can't scrub away the reality of what is about to happen but, somehow, I do feel better prepared to see my mum at the hospital.

I haven't managed to do much more than have a bath, but it's okay, I don't feel the need to push myself. I just want to take it all one step at a time. I'm sitting out on the veranda in a white fluffy bathrobe. I have swept my damp hair over to one side and I'm letting it dry naturally which, with this weather, won't take long.

My Diet Coke from the minibar is ice cold and it feels like such a big treat to be sipping this along with a few squares of Lindor chocolate. My view is serene, the gentle waves lapping against the creamy sand just thirty or so feet away, and for the first time since I arrived, my body doesn't feel so tight and tense.

Thank you so much, Jacob, I mumble to myself as I keep my eyes focused on the ocean in front of me. I do wish he was here. I didn't at first, I felt like I needed to be independent. I mean, I was married to Alex, I'm used to having to do the important things alone because he'd either be too unpredictable or just too drunk to remember to be there for me. But I wish I wasn't so stubborn. I know I felt I couldn't be around Jacob right now, because I'd be too caught up in the accusations Elle made about him being involved in some corrupt scheme to help vile Patrick stay out of prison. But honestly, as crazy as it may sound, right now, I really couldn't care less.

I wouldn't care if Elle accused him of being the next Ronnie and Reggie Kray – at this point, I just do not care. Because I know Jacob, I know there must be a reason behind the things Elle has said, and right now, I don't care what it is. I just wish I wasn't doing this alone; I wish he could be here to support me, in the way I always wished Alex could.

The gentle knock at the door pulls me out of my deep thoughts and back into the room.

"Coming," I call as I pull at my bathrobe a little bit, making sure I am fully covered. As I open the door, I'm greeted by the same friendly woman who showed me to my room.

"Ms Johnson, I'm so sorry to disturb you," she begins with a friendly smile. I still haven't caught her name yet and I really should.

"That's okay." I smile back. "I just finished having my Julia Roberts moment in the bathtub, so you haven't disturbed me in the slightest."

"Julia Roberts?"

"Yes, you know in *Pretty Woman*?"

"Oh, I see!" she blurts as she quickly makes the connection and laughs at the thought.

"Except, there is no Richard Gere in here." I playfully wink and she laughs a little more.

"Well, that is a shame, although I have come with some good news. I have just had Mr Jacob Jackson on the telephone. I hope you don't mind, but he was asking me how you were and if you had everything you need. I expressed a small concern that you didn't seem to have many bags or belongings with you."

"Uh-huh…" I listen eagerly, not entirely sure whether I'm supposed to be offended or flattered.

"And, well, he explained that you had a family emergency and had to leave in a hurry. Plus, he said you're quite ballsy and low maintenance…"

"Ballsy!?" I nearly choke on my Diet Coke. "Is Mr Jackson suggesting I don't really care about my appearance?"

"No, oh god no, he just said that when you have to be somewhere, you just go. You don't really stop to think about yourself, so he suspected you'd be unprepared."

My confused frown drops instantly and the thought of Jacob saying those things to a stranger makes me feel his warmth, even four thousand miles away.

"He has left some details with us and he said he'd like you to head to our shops in the main lobby and buy yourself whatever you need."

"Did he now?" I ask, with my brow arched.

"Yes. Oh, and he told me to tell you to fight your natural urges to be stubborn and just do it," she continues, although looking quite uncertain about whether she should say it or not.

I roll my eyes dramatically at his typical description of me.

"Wow, this just got a whole lot more like *Pretty Woman*, didn't it?"

She nods in response, mimicking my smile, before we both laugh at the realisation. Jacob has awkwardly taken the hypothetical role of Richard Gere in our little joke. Honestly, if I roll my eyes at the thought of him fussing over me again, they may stay stuck in the back of my head.

"Oh, wait. Before you go, what's your name?" I ask.

"Oh, it's Helen."

"Great, Helen. I'm Mia. Feel free to call me that and not Ms Johnson – it's weird being called that, I feel like my mum…"

I choke at the word. Mum.

"I'll look around the shops tomorrow Helen. I have somewhere to be this evening. But thank you so much for your help," I croak, before quickly closing the door on her.

I check the time on the alarm clock beside the bed. It's close to six o'clock now, the sun is going down and I promised Dr Garcia I'd be back. He said he'd be there until nine o'clock, but I need to get a move on. I can't hide in this hotel room forever. It's time to be brave, for Mum.

CHAPTER TEN

I throw on a little denim smock dress and notice that, after this, I only have one clean dress left. Jacob may have a fair point with how unprepared I can be – or low maintenance as he called it.

The sun has naturally dried my hair and left it with some cute beachy type waves as well as brightening up my blonde – it is much lighter than usual. I don't bother with make-up and I leave my hair to fall just as it already is. I put my feet into my coral-coloured sliders, grab my bag and head out of the hotel and down towards the taxi rank along the beach front.

I'm pleased that the taxi driver doesn't offer too much conversation because I don't have it in me to be sociable, especially now that I'm only minutes away from seeing my mum. I'm trying to mentally prepare myself to see her lying in a hospital bed with multiple machines around her keeping her alive. I try to think back to the hospital drama television shows I have seen over the years, like *Grey's Anatomy* and *Casualty.* I desperately try to recall scenes I have watched and use that to help me understand what I am about to see, but I'm finding it hard to imagine my own mum being the one lying there.

By the time I arrive at the hospital entrance, my anxiety has increased massively compared to how I was feeling back at the hotel. I can feel my feet starting to sweat in my sliders which is making it impossible to walk with any elegance and I'm pretty sure I'm visibly shaking, but I try hard to keep myself composed and hide it all as well as I possibly can.

As I approach the double doors and make my way into reception, I'm somewhat relieved to see Drea behind the desk, smiling away as she talks to someone on the phone. I like Drea, she has one of those comforting personalities, she's easy to warm to and talk with.

Her pretty smile drops quite quickly when she notices me approaching the desk, and she replaces it with a little nod, as if to offer sympathy. I guess she is now fully aware of my mum's fate and why I am back here at this time of evening.

"I'll ring you back tomorrow Sydney, something has come up and I must dash," she says politely before hanging up the phone and turning her attention to me.

"Mia, hi. How are you?"

"I'm okay. I think," I mutter with uncertainty. "I'm pleased to see you though."

A smile instantly spreads across her lips and I know she feels grateful that I have told her that.

"Well, I was due to leave at six, but I'm more than happy to stay with you, if you like?"

"That's so kind of you Drea," I say, feeling comforted by her efforts. "But I think it's best I do this alone. Plus, you won't want to see me cry. I'm an ugly crier." I attempt to joke to lighten the atmosphere. "But maybe if you're free tomorrow we could meet for a drink or something?"

"Yes!" Drea gasps as if it's a wonderful idea and she's surprised she didn't think of it first. "I'd love that! There's a little place called The Blue Sail, it's on pier one, by the markets. It's owned by my nana – we could meet there. She has the best seafood this side of town, although I'm probably a little biased! What do you think?"

I love how enthusiastically she tells me about her nana's restaurant and her seafood. I definitely find Drea to be the comfort that I need right now, and love that she doesn't at all seem to mind taking me under her wing, considering I'm just a relative of a patient. I'm sure she deals with loads of relatives, day in and day out, and I'm almost certain she doesn't take them all out for lunch. But I seem to have clicked with Drea and I think she appreciates that I'm alone out here and could really do with a friend.

"It's perfect Drea, it'll give me something to look forward to. Thank you so much," I answer tearily.

"Tomorrow will be a good day," Drea answers simply, full of confidence and wisdom. Again, the kind of comforting nature I really admire in her. "Although you won't be totally alone."

"Oh?"

"Yeah, a lady phoned earlier. She asked about your mum and she wanted to come by and say her goodbyes."

"Really? Did you catch her name at all?" I ask anxiously. I have no clue as to who that could be. Nobody has reached out to me about my mum. I didn't expect anyone to show up.

"I think she said her name was Megan. Does that ring a bell at all?"

"I don't think so." I shrug. "Did she say when she would be by?"

"She just said it would be later, when she got off work," Drea informs me as she gathers up her bag and keys, ready to leave the desk after a long day.

"Ah well, I guess I'll just wait and see then. I won't hold you up any longer. See you tomorrow."

"See you tomorrow." She smiles and reaches out to give my arm a gentle soothing squeeze before she disappears through the double doors.

I watch her walk away and I'm left with the familiar feeling of being alone again. But I remind myself that I can do this. I can do this.

"Ah, Ms Johnson, you made it in okay." I hear a deep voice call from behind me and swing round on my heel to see Dr Garcia waiting in the hallway, his hands in either pocket of his long white jacket and a smile on his face, although I can see the nervousness in his eyes. I am sure this is the part that all doctors dread. The part where they witness a loss, see your pain and, ultimately, are part of a moment that changes your life forever.

"Are you ready to see your mum?"

I anxiously sigh as if I suddenly needed a big breath of air and gulp it hard. I squeeze my hands to make fists in order to stop myself from shaking. I fiddle with my dress, pulling it down, adjusting it; it's fine as it is, but I can't help my fidgeting. I tuck my hair behind my ears before pulling down my dress again and then, finally, I take a step forward.

I nod and keep my head down towards the floor as I follow behind him. I watch as each step gets closer and closer to where she is. I can feel my heartbeat in my head. The palm of my hands feel tingly and sweaty and my legs begin to feel like jelly, but I keep taking a step forward. I keep going. I can do this.

CHAPTER ELEVEN

I hold my breath as I take one step inside her room. My eyes slowly flicker up to her bed. It's her. It's really her. My mum.

I let out a long exhale through my mouth as I quietly step towards her bed, almost as if I'm trying not to wake her up.

I'm somewhat calmer when I see that she actually does just look asleep. Her chocolate brown hair still has its usual bounce in it like it always does – this was Mum's signature look. When she was working on the ships, she liked to have a classy bouffant hairstyle, she said it made her feel glamourous. My dad would joke that it was her cruise ship alter-ego look. She'd finish it with thick eyeliner and a clear lip-gloss. A typical style for Mum's alter-ego. The majority of her make-up has faded now but she still has some black liner left on her lids. I don't think I ever took the time to realise just how beautiful Mum is. But I am carefully studying her now and she really is so beautiful.

Her hands are laid carefully by her side, and I reach out and place my hand over her warm skin. Her nails are beautifully manicured, a peachy colour with a silver rhinestone on each of her ring fingers. Subtle and very pretty.

The only part that doesn't feel like Mum is her mouth. The way she's been lying flat for so long has caused her lips to look droopy. Mum usually has plump lips, but I can't see any evidence of that now. They're also pale, like her skin tone. If I pretend hard enough that she still has her normal colour in her cheeks, I could trick myself into pretending she is just asleep, and not dying.

"Does it have to be right now?" I whisper, as I glance up to Dr Garcia.

"No, not at all. Please take your time to be with your mother. I will be in my office sorting out some of her paperwork. Let me know when you're ready," he answers before leaving me alone with Mum.

I awkwardly sit down on the chair beside her. I'm not really sure what to do now. I should have asked Dr Garcia if she can hear me, but I think maybe she can. At least that's what they say on *Grey's Anatomy*.

Without hesitation, I pull out my hairbrush from my bag and I softly comb it through Mum's hair, being careful not to take out the bouncy blow-dry look.
"There you go, Mum," I whisper as I admire how her hair falls gently around her face. "You were right about one thing: the Bahamas is absolutely beautiful," I continue. It's a weird feeling talking to someone you love who can't answer you, it brings a mixture of comfort and awkwardness. I like talking to her, of course I do, but I also wonder how insane I might look.

I notice something that I haven't noticed before and it takes me by surprise, but in a good way. On her wrist, she's wearing the watch that Dad bought her one Christmas. I think I was about thirteen or fourteen at the time, Dad was really excited because he had been saving up for a little while for it. Mum, however, wasn't totally sold on it. It was as horrendously awkward as it sounds. Dad waited with bated breath for a reaction that never came. Mum didn't gasp, or cry, or shout thank you a million times at the top of her lungs and parade around the room showing it off. She simply looked at it, looked at Dad, looked back at the watch and then said: "It's nice."

It was most certainly the biggest anti-climax I have ever witnessed. Poor Dad, he did look very deflated. But nonetheless, he dusted himself off as always and gave us the best Christmas he could.

It's odd because this watch stayed in Mum's jewellery box for as long as I can remember. I have never seen her wear it before – in fact, I didn't even know she so much as tried it on. But she is lying here now with it sitting comfortably on her wrist as if it had always been there.

Memories of our Christmases together and the story of this watch bring the tears to the surface. She was never very good at expressing herself, but she must have really loved the watch to be wearing it now after all these years.

"Oh Mum," I croak as I rest my head against her hand and allow myself a moment to let the tears come.

"Mia?" a female voice calls, startling me.

I pull away from Mum's hand and quickly compose myself. A tall lady with long blonde curly hair is standing in the doorway.

"Yes?"

"Oh my god. Mia! You're even prettier in person!" she squeals excitedly as she rushes over and wraps her arms around me before I even have the chance to ask who she is. This has to be Megan.

"Thank you…"

"Megan. I'm Megan," she proudly says as she fills in my blanks.

"Wow, you sound just like Dolly Parton!" I blurt out before I can stop myself.

"Okay, that's weird because that is the exact same thing your mother said to me when I first met her! Look…" she says as she pulls up the sleeve of her white cardigan and shows me the goosebumps on her arm. "That's given me the heebie-jeebies! That's spooky."

Megan has a real country style look: she literally looks like she could have walked out of a cowboy movie. She's wearing white ankle boots with a denim skirt, a tank top and a white cardigan. Her hair just might be bigger and bouncier than my mum's – and that's truly saying something.

She has a thick American accent but a real southern one, like Alabama or Tennessee, somewhere like that. If you closed your eyes, you might really think Dolly Parton was in the room.

"Oh, my..." she says as her eyes focus on Mum behind me. Her shoulders drop down, her bubbly demeanour softens and this chatty woman has suddenly been silenced.

"God, I usually trust your plans, but please, not my Thelma. It's not her goddamn time," she says in a strained voice. I notice that, just like mine, her eyes are now filled with tears too.

"Thelma?" I question gently.

"Yep. That's my Thelma. And I'm her Louise. It's what they used to call us on board because we were inseparable. But we had a lot in common, you know? So we clicked, and then we became soul sisters."

"That's lovely but, and I don't want to sound rude, I honestly don't recall my mum ever mentioning you?"

I feel awful saying it, but this is the first time I have ever heard of Megan and I'm confused. She's referencing Thelma and Louise, so they must have been so close. Why did I not hear her name before now?

Megan just smiles and nods. She doesn't seem at all surprised that I've not heard her name.

"Your mum used to say that you didn't like to listen much about her life on the cruises and she didn't want to upset you."

"She said that?"

"Yeah. She knew you found her job tough as a kid and she felt guilty as hell. She thought it best to keep boat chat to a minimum."

"Oh," is all I manage to follow up with.

But now I'm curious to learn what else my mum may have been doing in her life that she didn't feel she could tell me about.

"Fancy some coffee? Canteen is upstairs. We can chat for a bit if you like?" Megan offers, seemingly aware that I'm struggling to make sense of a friendship I never knew about.

"Yeah, I'd like that." I nod and give Mum's cheek a little kiss before heading through the door with Megan close behind.

CHAPTER TWELVE

Even the canteen has potted palm trees in the corners. It seems wherever you go here, even just a plain old hospital canteen, everything has been given an injection of their exotic lifestyle.

Megan heads to the counter and orders us both a latte while I save us a table by the large window. The sun has very nearly set for the night and the sky is a beautiful mixture of dark orange with streaks of pearly pink and lilac; I have always appreciated the beauty of a sunset, but this is particularly stunning.

"I never get bored of seeing that." Megan smiles as she places two lattes on the table but keeps her eyes fixed on the sunset.

"It's definitely something special." I nod and take a sip from the paper cup.

"Oh Mia, I truly am sorry about your mum. I have been selfish. I may have lost my Thelma but you're losing your mum and that doesn't compare to my pain."

"It's okay..." I interrupt, hoping to lessen her guilt. "Sadly, we weren't that close."

Megan stares at me softly but looks as if her heart has just dropped.

"Mia..." Megan whispers as she reaches for my hand. "I think you were closer than you think. Your mum just had..." She pauses nervously, trying to find the right words. "There were things she wanted to protect you from that kept her away. I promised her that if anything were to happen to her, I would tell you all about it."

"Protect *me* from?"

"Yes, honey. Your mum had some battles. Now I truly believe God doesn't give us anything that we cannot deal with and your mum was no exception to that. She dealt with it all as well as she could, but it came at a price for her."

I admire how Megan uses her faith to comfort me before she has even explained anything to me, but the more she tiptoes around the facts, the more anxious I become.

"It's okay Megan. I can handle whatever it is, please tell me straight."

"I met your mum around seven years ago. We both worked on the ship, but I hadn't ever bumped into her before, not until we both ended up in the infirmary on the lower deck. I'm a receptionist you see, I greet people as they get on board, deal with financial things, excursions, all sorts really. And, as you know, your mum was a performer. So, she'd usually be asleep all day and awake all night entertaining the crowd. She did a wonderful job too; she has the most beautiful voice."

I agree with a nod, although I haven't heard my mum sing since I was a little girl. She'd sing to help me fall asleep at night. I would miss it a lot when she left us again, but I couldn't tell you what she sounds like now.

"Anyway, I was in the infirmary because I tripped in my cabin one morning and really hurt my wrist, so I was getting it checked out. That's when I saw your mum, curled up into a ball on the bed; she was white as a sheet, and clearly crying, but trying her best to hide it. I didn't want to impose and ask her what was wrong. I almost walked away, but then I heard her mumble something and it stopped me in my tracks."

"What did she mumble?" I ask as I lean closer.

"*Not again, please not again.*" Megan looks down at her cup; she looks emotional recalling that memory. I can feel how much she cared for my mum just from how she repeated those words.

"Once I heard that, I couldn't just walk away and pretend I didn't hear her pain. I had to stop. I asked her what was wrong, and she just stared blankly into space, she didn't answer me. That's when Dominic came in, he's one of the nurses on board; he pleaded with her to allow him to take her to the hospital for a proper check over when we docked. But she refused. He then gently told her off, you know like as a friend, not in a nasty way. He told her she couldn't keep doing this. She agreed. She said she was sorry but that it wasn't that easy. She said she went to bed okay and woke up in hell again. She said she was scared. And that's when I knew, because I have been there. Do you know much about mental health Mia?"

Oh my god. Did my mum have mental health problems and I didn't even know?

"Yes. A fair bit. I struggle with anxiety myself and I've been around other people who have had demons to deal with. I understand it. But I had no idea about Mum..."

"Your mum was battling with bouts of manic depression and panic attacks. One day she'd be on stage, singing her heart out and her aura would literally spill over with joy and charisma. Other days, she said the black fog was back. She couldn't see herself living in pain anymore and sometimes she'd do silly things like take a cocktail of painkillers and hard liquor. She'd stop herself before any real damage could happen and that's when she'd be in the most pain, because that's when she wanted to live – she just didn't want to live under the black fog."

"I had no idea..." I say as I drop my head into my hands.

"Honey, your mum didn't want you to know. That's why she stayed away on the cruise ships. She was terrified that one day you might witness one of her bad days and she said she couldn't allow that to happen. The guilt would have been too much for her to bear."

"But I could have helped her. Why couldn't she have told me as an adult?" I ask desperately, and Megan is already shaking her head with a sympathetic smile.

"She didn't want you to help her. She wanted you to be happy. She felt strongly that this was one thing she never wanted you to have to worry about."

I think this is the first time I have ever felt so much compassion for my mum. Usually I'm mad at her for not feeling compassionate enough to be a better wife to my dad or a better mum to me. Now I'm sitting here and for the first time ever, so much about my upbringing and childhood makes sense. It helps me so much to know this; I have such a different understanding. It still breaks my heart that I didn't know before now, but I admire my mum so much for actually trying to protect us. I had no idea she loved us this much.

"But she had you though?" I ask. "To help her, I mean."

"Oh yes! Your mum and I clicked from that day on. I didn't leave her side for the next few days, not until the black fog started to lift for her. That's when I explained to your mum that I have bipolar disorder. So I know a few things about unstable moods!" She laughs. "We helped each other a lot. I became her rock and she became mine."

"I'm grateful she had you…"

Megan smiles gratefully and reaches out to give my hand another little affectionate squeeze.

"Have you seen the film *Thelma and Louise*?" she asks.

"It's one of my favourite movies," I answer, recalling the many times I have sat curled up with ice-cream and watched it.

"Well, you know the end scene where Thelma says to Louise:

'Let's keep going'? Your mum and I would use that line for our mental health. Whenever one of us was struggling, we'd just look at each other and say it."

With a smile, she sips at her latte.

"Shall we go and sit with her? I miss her," Megan whispers and I get to my feet immediately.

"Let's go."

CHAPTER THIRTEEN

To my surprise, Dr Garcia is sitting next to my mum when we return to her room.

"I'm afraid we will need to start soon," he gently informs us.

Oh god, this is it. I quickly rummage around in my bag and pull out the crystal I got from the lovely woman at the market.

I perch carefully on the edge of the bed and my hands tremble nervously as I break the crystal into two parts.

I need to break down in tears right now, I need to cuddle my mum whilst I sob and tell her how much I love her and how much I'm going to miss her, but I can't, not with Dr Garcia and Megan in the room. I don't know them well enough to allow myself to be so vulnerable.

I place one crystal in the palm of her hand and close her fingers around it.

"Is she okay to go with this in her hand?" I squeak.

Dr Garcia nods sympathetically as I take a deep breath and keep Mum's hand in mine.

"Thank you, Mum. I know now that you were only trying to protect me, and I love you for it."

I hold the other crystal tightly in my hand and stare down at it. This half safely in my hand and the other half tucked away with Mum.

It's strange to think it, but I can't help but feel that this is probably the way Mum would have chosen to go if she had a say: somewhere exotic, hot and beautiful with her friend and her daughter beside her bed and a crystal from the local stall in her hand. Somehow, this just feels like Mum's perfect goodbye.

I suddenly have the urge to tell her all about Jacob and how I can actually understand a bit more about how she got caught up with some Irish guy on the ship. That's obviously different because she wasn't in love with him like I am with Jacob, but I get it. I get that someone came along who offered her a bit of adventure or excitement, whatever it was. I understand that it doesn't make her a bad person.

"Mum…" I whisper ever so softly as I lean over closely to her ear. "We're more alike than we ever knew. I love you," I manage before giving her a gentle kiss on the cheek and pulling away to give Dr Garcia space to take out the tubes.

"Are we ready?" Dr Garcia asks and Megan and I nod simultaneously.

I watch as he carefully removes a large tube from Mum's throat and unclips the monitor around her fingertips. He talks us through what he is doing as he does it, but his words are like a distant mumble in the background; I can barely focus on a word he is saying. I'm too busy watching intently and praying that Mum will take a breath and show us hope, but instead, and as expected, I'm watching her slip away.

It's quick, so quick, and somehow that shows me quite clearly that my poor mum was only hanging on by a thread and now she's finally drifting off into a deep sleep, finally at peace.

"Best friends forever," Megan whimpers from behind me. I turn to look at her and I instantly ache at the lost expression on her face. "Save a seat up there for me, won't you?" she adds.

Megan looks like she also wants to fall apart but I think she's keeping a lid on it just for me.

It must be painful for her; she has been with my mum almost

every single day. How do you go from that to nothing?

"I'm sorry," Megan says remorsefully. "I'm going on like a selfish idiot and she's your mum after all." A tear falls down her cheek.

"No! Not at all. Please don't apologise. I was literally just thinking about how you and Mum were together every day and how hard this must be for you. She's my mum, yes, but she's your best friend. Please don't ever be sorry."

Megan walks over to me and hugs me tight. We stay hugging each other tightly until Dr Garcia gently announces her time of death.

"9:14pm."

Megan and I pull away from each other to take one last look at Mum.

It's a surreal moment, somehow. I already know this moment will be a blur when I look back on it. It feels like I'm in a dream or watching this happen to somebody else. It just doesn't feel real.

"I feel like I just want to go home and pull out every photo album we have and look back at all our memories," I mutter, aching for her already.

"There's a bar next door. How about we get something stronger than a coffee this time and have a little toast?" Megan suggests, her voice sounding positive but her bloodshot eyes telling the truth.

I nod appreciatively. "That'll be really nice."

CHAPTER FOURTEEN

We head over the road to a bar called The Daiquiri Shack, which is as cool as it sounds. The whole bar is filled with giant bowls of fresh fruit and each cocktail is made up with the ripest fruits, blended up into smoothies and then a lashing of vodka or tequila added.

I rarely drink tequila because it just sounds like a hangover from hell waiting to happen, but tonight a hangover is the least of my worries.

Megan and I aren't shy with our orders. We're ordering a shot with almost every drink and what started out as sensible and serious speeches with each shot, as we toasted Mum, have ended up with us mentioning any ridiculous reason we can think of just to throw back a shot.

"To the time Mum tried to give me a haircut and all the kids at school laughed at me for at least a week!" I screech as I raise my shot above my head.

"Cheers!" Megan laughs as we both knock back yet another shot of tequila.

"Oh my god! Wait, I've got the best one!" Megan screams as she starts climbing on her chair. "I gotta get on the chair for this one!" she giggles.

I have no idea what she's about to say but her enthusiasm has me laughing hard. Well that and the numerous tequilas.

"Here's to my best friend, who once took a pee on my bedroom floor because she was so drunk, she thought she was in the bathroom!" Megan announces loudly and we both roar with laughter.

"Oh my god!" I shout before throwing back another tequila shot.

Megan orders us a banana rum smoothie and another two shots of tequila.

"Is the room spinning for you?" I giggle.

"Not enough for my liking!" Megan responds and hands me another cocktail smoothie.

"Okay girl, it's your turn! What are we toasting to?"

I take my shot glass and think momentarily before something comes to mind.

"A-ha!" I announce. "Here's to my mum who had a one-week affair with an Irish man!" I shout and throw back the shot hard.

My face screws up as the liquid burns my throat and I realise when I open my eyes again that Megan is just sat gawping at me with her untouched shot still in her hand.

"What?" I ask, bemused.

"Are you talking about Cillian?" Megan asks curiously.

"Cillian? I don't know. Mum didn't remember his name; she barely knew his accent! It was just some brief affair."

"Yeah, that was Cillian. But it wasn't a one-week affair."

"Yes, it was," I say a bit abruptly. "She told me."

"Okay." Megan shrugs and throws back her shot.

"Wait. What is okay?"

"I'm just agreeing with you."

"Yeah, to keep me happy by the looks of it. But that's not the truth is it?"

Megan shakes her head.

"I'm realising now that your mum said a lot more things than I thought to spare your feelings," Megan informs me.

"But you weren't there? This was all before I was born."

"It's a long story," Megan says and sips at her banana smoothie.

"Tell me, Megan, please?"

"I just don't want to put your mum in any bad light. That's not fair. She loved you and only ever wanted you to be proud of her."

"I won't judge Megan, I assure you. I'm in no position to judge anymore, that's for sure…"

Megan's brow arches inquisitively.

"I'll save that story for another day! Tonight is about Mum." I blush awkwardly.

"Okay. Well, you're right. The initial affair was only a week and then your mum called the whole thing off. She didn't want to, but she felt awful for what she had done and decided she didn't want to do this to your dad anymore."

I nod to show I'm listening. Listening would be an understatement though; I'm fully invested in this story now. I'm learning so much about my mum thanks to Megan.

"This guy was different. Your mum used to say that he made her feel invincible. Seen was the word she used most, yeah; she'd say he made her feel seen. Well, he wasn't ready to give up either. He wrote her letters, sent her flowers, told her he would happily marry her in a heartbeat if it was his commitment she needed. He asked her to move to Cork in Ireland with him. He pretty much offered her everything, but each time, she said no. She felt strongly that she had to make everything up to your dad. She wanted to be a better wife. It was bad enough she worked away so much, but she couldn't have this guilt too."

"Wow," is all I manage to contribute. A few months ago, this story would have broken my heart for how my dad would have been affected by it. But now, I can see it from the other side too, and I feel sympathy for Mum.

"So, your mum and dad were on much better terms and your mum was working her last month before she left for maternity leave. Back then, your mum was one of the crew members who would stand at the ship's entrance and greet new passengers as they boarded. And well, you can only imagine her face when she saw Cillian boarding."

"NO!" I gasp.

"Yep. He booked the cruise purposefully to look for your mum."

"I can't imagine how shocked she must have been!"

"Probably not as shocked as Cillian was when he saw her pregnant belly!"

"Shit, yeah!" I gasp again and we both burst out laughing at the thought.

"From what I understand, after the initial shock, he met up with your mum in her cabin later that night and proposed."

"Proposed!?" I squeal excitedly. "This is crazy! I can't believe all this happened!"

"Yep! Let me tell you, her heart still dropped when she told me she turned him down, again. Even after all these years. She battled majorly between her head and her heart back then. In the end, her head won."

"You don't think my dad was her heart?" I ask, a little offended.

Megan shrugs awkwardly.

"She said she didn't deserve your dad. He was the best father she could have ever picked for you and he loved your mum no matter what. She said he deserved better from her and that's what she did. She tried to be better for him and for you."

"What happened to Cillian?"

"Cillian eventually accepted it, but he didn't give up fully for a long time – he continued writing your mum letters and letting her know that he'd always love her. She would occasionally write back, just to let him know that she was happy and doing well and that she hoped the same for him." Megan's gaze directly meets mine. "And that's why I hate the word affair to describe what those two had. It was so much more."

Like Jacob, I mutter under my breath, but Megan hears.

"Jacob?" she quizzes.

"Yes. A married man I completely fell in love with in what was one of the most random, whirlwind experiences of my life. Everything from start to finish is so unlike me – I never knew I had this side of me and, as much as I tried, every inch of me has been consumed by him. It's been full on from the word go: it's been intense, sexy, scary, exciting, passionate, dramatic and an adventure."

"Sounds amazing." Megan winks.

"It is." I sigh as I suddenly miss Jacob so much.

CHAPTER FIFTEEN

After a couple more tequila slammers, it seems wise to start making my way back to the hotel considering I can barely see or keep my eyes open. The world seems to sway around me as I step out of the taxi and head towards the hotel lobby.

"Good evening, have you had a nice night?" a young man asks me from behind the desk as I stagger over.

"Terrific, thanks," I slur. "We went to The Daiquiri Shack, you know by the beach, had a few tequilas, a little dance; and had these amazing banana rum smoothies. Oh! And my mum died."

The man's smile instantly drops and there is a confused and awkward silence. I definitely know how to make people suddenly feel uncomfortable.

"Sorry, I overshare when I'm drunk." I shake my head dramatically. "I'm going to go now. Can I have some room service?"

"Yes, ma'am, of course. What would you like?"

"French fries please. And a huge margarita pizza, like the biggest you have, ever. Ooh, and a banana split!" I squeal excitedly like a child in a candy shop.

"Sure, we'll have it brought up to you shortly." He smiles, seemingly a lot more relaxed now that I'm not talking about my dead mum.

It's not easy to walk in a straight line after tequila that's for sure. I keep my hand pressed against the wall to keep me steady as the usually very short walk feels like a mammoth trek.

The thought of a greasy cheesy pizza keeps me as focused as I can possibly be. My stomach feels oddly empty despite copious smoothies. When I make my way to my room, I strip off immediately down to my underwear. I forgot to leave the air-conditioning on when I went out, so the room is humid to say the least.

I pull my hair out of its ponytail and allow it to freely fall. It feels so nice to take everything off and just relax like a starfish across the huge bed which has been carefully turned down by the maids already.

Moments later a gentle knock sounds against my door and I totally forget that I am only in underwear until a young porter blushes awkwardly as he wheels in my food.

"Oh crap!" I shout as I hit my head with the palm of my hand. "I totally forgot to get some change for a tip."

"That's quite alright madam," the porter replies, looking desperate to leave as quickly as possible.

"I can flash you a boob. Would that make us even?" I slur, before giggling at his growing embarrassment.

"That's quite alright ma'am," he croaks nervously before spinning round and heading for the door.

As soon as the door is closed behind him, I hurriedly grab the pizza box and head for the veranda. It smells delicious. The pizza looks so fresh and my mouth waters as I break a slice away; but as I bring it to my lips, I suddenly feel a weird lump in my throat.

My mouth waters more but no longer in a good way. I realise my heart is racing and my stomach is doing flips.

My mum's gone. I can't eat this!

And with that thought I'm running to the bathroom as I feel my body preparing to throw up. I make it just in time, just as every smoothie and tequila shot of the evening makes a gross reappearance.

My head rests against the toilet seat after I stop vomiting. My stomach is painful, and my chest is burning. I feel so vulnerable. So alone.

I need Jacob.

Carefully, I pull myself to my feet and walk slowly back into the bedroom to find my phone.

My heart sinks a little when I realise Jacob hasn't tried to call or text me today. I know I told him I needed space, but I didn't expect him to listen.

My thumb quickly finds his number and I anxiously press my ear against the phone and wait for it to ring.

Within seconds it goes straight to his voicemail and I immediately feel sicker and more anxious than I was moments ago. His phone always rings. I've never known it to go to voicemail. Why would it be off?

Oh god, what if my life is just too depressing right now and he can't be bothered with the stress of it all and he has blocked me?

What if me being away has made him think differently?

Like, what if he has decided it was just a fling and not love after all?

I must admit, I feel like a crazy person as I dial again and again, hoping for a different outcome, but each time his phone goes straight to voicemail.

The alcohol clouds my thinking and somehow, I have gone from anxious to angry. How dare he turn his phone off in my time of need?

"Jacob!" I screech into the phone as it goes to voicemail for the sixth time. "Where the fuck are you? I need you right now and you're not there for me. I hope you're not thinking you can just pop in and out of my life when it suits, because I won't accept that. You can't just put me up in a five-star hotel and think that is love because it's not. Love is being there for that person through all of the good and all of the bad! Do you get that?"

I pause as I pace my room angrily.

"Okay, okay, okay." I roll my eyes drunkenly as word vomit appears this time. "So, you may be the best sex I have ever had. So what? So, you may be the only man to give me an orgasm without me having to finish myself off. But don't let that go to your head because I have a vibrator that does the exact same thing and that doesn't come with complications. So, so, yeah!" I babble, ridiculously incoherent.

The next thing I know my head hits the pillow and I drop the phone beside me. My heavy eyes close and I give in to the exhaustion and stresses of today.

CHAPTER SIXTEEN

Why must alcohol punish us like this? All I wanted was a care-free evening to numb the pain and to party like I didn't have a care in the world – and it worked for a few hours.

But of course, by the morning, the alcohol has completely turned against you and you're waking up to nothing but regret and a bad head.

It was a huge effort just to crawl out of bed for a wee this morning; my head was so heavy and foggy and every time I stood up, I felt like the world was spinning around me. My throat was scratchy and dry, and my eyes felt heavy and tired. I definitely didn't feel as fresh waking up as I hoped I would.

If it wasn't for my plans with Drea today, I would have turned over, pulled the white linen sheets up high over my head and stayed there for the rest of the day. Thank goodness for Drea, because I know I need to push through and get out of bed. Wallowing won't help me.

I still haven't heard from Jacob, not even a text message, and I'm trying to distract myself from worrying about it so much, but it's not easy.

I'm wearing my last clean dress now, a cute white tea dress, so light and airy. Perfect for today seeing as it's supposed to be the hottest day of the month so far, at least that's what I heard on the weather channel whilst I was fixing my hair this morning. I either need to find a launderette today or give in to my stubbornness and get a few extra items in the lobby shops.

It feels weird though to go and buy myself clothes when I'm not the one paying for them, especially when I haven't even spoken to Jacob recently. Would he even mind if I still went shopping? I really don't know right now.

The walk down to The Blue Sail restaurant is idyllic and relaxing. I'm so pleased Drea invited me out to meet her. I needed this more than I could have known.

If I wasn't so distracted by everything that was going on, I would have remembered to bring my camera with me so I could capture this beautiful island and all it has to offer.

As I get closer to the pier and reach The Blue Sail, I smile at how perfect it looks – if you googled 'picturesque Caribbean restaurant' this literally looks like the image you would expect to see.

Drea must have spotted me because she comes rushing out of the entrance and darts towards me for a big sympathetic hug. I guess I'd best get used to those for a while.

"I spoke to the hospital this morning and they told me the news," she says whilst she keeps her arms wrapped around me.

She doesn't need to say anything else; her tight hug is enough.

It's strange how a person offering you their sympathy makes you want to cry so much more than you did moments ago. It's like they give you the green light to let your emotions spill over. But even though Drea is wonderful and comforting, I find it hard to cry about Mum in front of her.

"You probably haven't eaten much, come inside. My nana has whipped up some local cuisine. You'll love it!" she says with her wide smile, showing her perfectly white teeth.

The restaurant is empty – it seems the chef is cooking for just me and Drea.

"It's usually a lot busier than this but we aren't opening yet. I thought it would be nice just to have a quiet catch up first."

"You didn't have to do that for me," I stutter in shock, feeling some guilt that she has gone so far to accommodate me.

"That's what friends are for!" she smiles again and playfully nudges me.

Drea hands me a non-alcoholic pina colada and explains enthusiastically what all the dishes are as they are brought out to us. Most of it is fish and a lot of spicy rice. It is absolutely delicious and very filling. The first few mouthfuls were hard to swallow though – I had forgotten how sick I was last night, and only remembered when my throat felt so scratchy and sore when I swallowed.

Drea does most of the talking which is a relief because I know I don't have too much good conversation to offer right now. Unless of course she wants to hear how I got absolutely wrecked last night, ordered a tonne of room service, threw up when it finally arrived and then cried myself to sleep.

Instead, I gratefully sip my refreshing virgin pina colada as Drea tells me stories about some of the things she's got up to living on the Bahamas. She tells me that a couple of years ago a hurricane wiped out around fifty houses and how the entire community came together to help rebuild everything for those who had lost so much.

She talks so passionately about the locals and her lifestyle here. I'm starting to think she should be an estate agent instead of a receptionist because she's seriously making me want to pack up and leave my suburban home and live the island life.

Soon dessert is brought out and it pretty much feels like it's just blown my head off with one bite.

"You like rum cake?" Drea asks.

"I'm not sure if I have ever had it. It certainly has a lot of rum in it doesn't it?"

And by a lot I mean the entire cake is drenched in rum. I may as well have a straw and be drinking it.

"Well, we love our rum here!" Drea giggles as I cough and splutter between mouthfuls.

By the time I finish my dessert, I feel different. Any energy I had has gone and I suddenly feel really sad. The kind of sad where you just can't be around people anymore. You just want to hide in your bed, maybe listen to some music, watch a film, eat chocolate and have that time to cry to yourself and rest. That's what my body is telling me I need.

Usually, I would try and suck it up and stay for another hour to be polite, but I feel too drained to even try that.

I quickly explain to Drea that I have come over very tired all of a sudden and that I think I need to go back to the hotel and rest.

Drea is ever so sweet and understanding about it, just as I expected she would be. I offer some money towards all the food, but she vigorously declines so much as a penny. She assures me this was her treat.

I promise her that we'll meet again before I fly back home, whenever that might be.

I walk back quickly, eagerly anticipating the moment I feel the air-conditioning against my skin and the comfort of the giant double bed.

I walk through the hotel, grabbing some banana bread and watermelon from the lobby on my way. With any luck, I won't need to leave my room again now until tomorrow.

As my key card flashes green and my door swings open, I'm startled by what I see.

"Jacob?" I gasp

Jacob is perched on the edge of the bed, his hair slightly messy from his long plane journey.

His white shirt is unbuttoned and his tie unknotted and open. He peers up from the ground and holds my stare as he runs his thumb across his jawline and towards his lips.

"Are you happy to see me?" he asks, but we both know the answer.

I run my hands down my dress awkwardly, hoping I look as good as he does.
"You look like you came straight from the office?"

"I pretty much did. I couldn't sit at home any longer, not whilst I knew everything you were going through. So, I'm here. I'm here and I'll do whatever I can to help you. Just tell me what you need, and I'll do it."

I drop my bag on the floor and close the door behind me, but I don't lose his eye contact.

"I want you to fuck me," I breathe as I take a step closer to the edge of the bed. My emotions are all over the place but the one thing that is clear is how much I want him.

Jacob briefly smirks and looks away, almost as if he is blushing. But then he stands up, towering over me, and bites his bottom lip as he looks hungrily down at me.

"I didn't necessarily mean that," he assures me, but I can see the temptation is growing inside of him.

"I know," I whisper, "but I need you."

Jacob's eyes narrow as he bends his head towards my face. "Tell me what you want."

"Undress me," I say as I hold my breath in anticipation.

The tips of Jacob's fingers gently graze either side of my thighs as he begins to lift up my dress, revealing my white lace underwear and exposed breasts. The air-conditioning can do nothing to stop the heat that is engulfing us now.

"No bra?" Jacob breathes as he drops my dress beside us and runs his thumb gently over my nipple.

I tug impatiently at his white shirt as I release it from his black belt. I want him now, I need him.

"Miss me?" Jacob asks smugly. He knows the answer, so instead of responding, I choose to turn things up a notch and surprise him. I grab his hand and push it hard against the damp lace of my knickers, allowing him to feel how wet I have become.

"Mia…" he whispers eagerly, "tell me what you want next."

I feel so wanted and so powerful as Jacob watches me glide over to the mini bar and grab a small bottle of champagne. I make my way over to the desk and pull out the chair. I perch on the desk and spread my legs apart, resting one leg on the chair. Jacob watches on intently.

I carefully unscrew the cap from the champagne bottle and arch my back as I slowly tip out the contents and let it spill over my stomach and down in between my legs.

"Taste it," I command.

Jacob immediately comes and sits on the chair. I move my leg for him and relax it over his shoulder instead, leaving my other leg parted. He watches my body glistening from the champagne but concentrates closely on my folds; I gasp as he lowers his mouth onto me.

My body jerks back into a more curved arch as I push against his tongue. I keep one hand on the desk and use the other to grab hold of his messy hair and roughly push him deeper into me. I know he likes it because he brings his hands up and grips my hips tightly and excitedly.

I can't deny this chemistry between us, I never have. Just one touch from Jacob and my skin feels inflamed. My body throbs helplessly for him. I throw my head back and whine delightedly at the feelings Jacob is giving me. His tongue is swirling and flicking hard against my most sensitive area, and my heart is pounding hard against my chest as I feel him bringing me closer to the edge.

I muster up enough strength to pull myself up and reach down to his thickening cock.

"I need you now, inside of me, now," I whimper desperately, my words instantly exciting Jacob as he stands straight up and grabs my legs tightly around his waist. He pushes me back down onto the desk as he slams himself hard inside of me, causing me to groan loudly with pleasure. He slides his hands around to the small of my back and uses that grip to push me down harder onto his length.

I feel my cheeks redden as I sense myself getting ready to explode all over his solid erection.

Jacob's thrusts speed up and our sweaty bodies grind hard together just as we both reach a beautiful orgasm. My body lies motionless underneath Jacob's chiselled body. I'm exhausted, and I'm satisfied.

CHAPTER SEVENTEEN

I wake up thirsty and a little groggy; it's been a stressful time and I think the emotional rollercoaster is starting to catch up with me.

I gently slip out of the bed, careful not to wake Jacob, and grab a nice cold bottle of still water from the minibar. I press it against my forehead momentarily – the cool condensation from the bottle is refreshing. I decide to sit outside on the veranda. The stars are beautiful here – well, they're beautiful everywhere but they seem so big here. I guess when you're not close to a busy polluted city like London, it's easier to see the natural beauty around us that we often don't notice.

I glance back at Jacob who is lying on his front; the dim light from the moon highlights his shoulder blades beautifully and that image alone is enough to make my heart skip a beat. I have so many strong feelings for Jacob, more than I have had for anyone. From the way he makes me feel so safe when I'm around him to the way he excites me with our passion. But there is one thing niggling away at me. Elle told me to ask him why Patrick isn't in prison and that he raped a woman. Raped. God, the word makes me feel sick. The thought of any man forcing himself onto a woman is stomach curdling; and to think it could have been me next.

So, what is it that Elle means? How is Jacob involved? I don't know. Should I know? Do I even want to know?

I had told myself that this trip was going to be about my mum only. I simply didn't have the head space for any other issues. I still don't, really, but curiosity is getting the best of me. Plus, we are here on an island together so whatever the answer is, we have no choice but to talk through it. Neither of us can run away from each other right now.

Every woman has a slightly crazier version of herself tucked away inside. We don't like to admit it, but we do. Some people see it as a negative, especially men when they like to refer to women as 'crazy bitches' or something similar. I, however, see it as a positive. The slightly crazy alter ego protects me. She gives me a strength when I need it. She's a badass. She's the Sasha Fierce to Beyoncé. And she's telling me there is no time like the present.

I creep back into the bedroom and stand at the end of the bed. He looks so peaceful sleeping that I nearly change my mind about waking him up. But it's time. I need those answers.

"Oops!" I over-dramatically gasp as I accidentally – totally on purpose – drop my glass bottle of water on the floor, causing a loud shattering sound which instantly wakes up a confused and semi-conscious Jacob.

"Oh good, you're awake," I casually say as if I didn't just plan that.

"Well I am now, are you okay? What happened?" he croaks whilst rubbing his eyes.

"I'm fine. I just need to know the truth. I can't sleep properly because there's far too much on my mind."

"Truth about what?"

"I think you know what," I say gently but firmly which seems enough to jog Jacob's memory because he is now sitting up with a serious expression on his face.

"But Mia, surely this isn't the time. Your mum…"

"Jacob, please don't use my mum's death to get out of discussing this," I snap.

"Hey!" Jacob instantly snaps back as he darts out of bed and stands in front of me. He grabs hold of my waist with authority and spins me round to face him.

"Firstly, I'm not trying to get out of anything Mia, I'm not a coward thank you. Secondly, you are my priority right now and I just didn't want to add to your upset with any shit from my past. But if right now is when you want to discuss it, at three o'clock in the morning, then let's fucking discuss it."

Jacob quickly pulls on his black boxers and heads out to the veranda with his own bottle of water.

"Before I begin, you need to know something Mia. I'm not at all proud of this. It's not just a minor regret that I've moved on from, it's something that's haunted me for a very long time. I know what Patrick is like, which is why I lost it with him that night – he wasn't going to do it to you too, no fucking way," Jacob breathes through gritted teeth.

"I'll try to understand," I answer honestly. I can't promise that I definitely will, but I know I want to.

Jacob looks scared. His eyes flicker uncomfortably from my face down to his hands as he fidgets. I can see the dread in his face.

"I'll start from the very beginning. Patrick and my dad grew up together. They lived just streets apart and ended up at the same schools and then went onto the same university. They were inseparable. Their families mixed often, they were a very close and tight-knit unit. They looked out for each other. Anyway, my dad really struggled with the pressure at university and didn't cope with his stress very well. A few of his roommates introduced him to the racing, you know, gambling on horses?"

I nod intently.

"It was fun at first, my dad found it a good distraction from all his worries. He won a few times and said it was a cool buzz, and then they'd go and celebrate down the pub with the winnings. It seemed harmless and fun; he had no idea that it could become so addictive. In a matter of months, my dad couldn't get the same buzz unless he was gambling with big money. Only, I'm sure you don't need me to tell you that with every win there's always a loss and my dad struggled to keep his head above water. He knew he was in trouble when he realised he'd gambled away his entire university funds. He panicked and thought he could earn it back before my grandad found out. But in order to do it, he needed more funds. He must have been desperate because the first chance he got, he stole a very important heirloom from my grandad's office. An antique solid gold pocket watch. He sold it and gambled again in the hope that he'd earn something back, but his luck had run out. He lost the lot."

"Jesus…" I whisper.

"It gets worse. A little while after that, my dad was back home having dinner with his parents when my grandad decided he couldn't wait any longer, he wanted to pass the heirloom down to my dad to show how proud he was of his university results. When my grandad went to the office to retrieve it and couldn't find it, he went into a pure panic. He was convinced a member of staff must have taken it and the idea he might never see it again was just too much for him to bear. That night, he suffered a heart attack."

My hands come up to my mouth in shock. This story is devastating and Jacob's face explaining it isn't much better.

"He survived, don't worry. The doctors said it was minor, but it was terrifying. After that, my grandad lost all his confidence and stopped leaving the house so much. He was too worried about his health. I think the doctors called it agoraphobia. My dad felt awful but his problems weren't over yet. My grandad was still to learn that my dad had no university funds left. Although my grandad was wealthy, a lot of his finances were tied up in his estate and his land. The stress of finding another huge lump sum could cause him another heart attack, at least that's what my dad feared. In the end, he turned to Patrick for help.

"Which…" Jacob continues with a heavy sigh, "may have turned out to be more bad than good."

"Did Patrick get the money for him?"

"Yes. For Patrick's birthday, his dad had bought him an Aston Martin, but when Patrick found out what had been going on with my dad, he sold his car straight away. He came up with some bullshit excuse to his own dad that he didn't like the colour and he gave sixty thousand pounds to my dad to put back in the bank, so that my grandad would never find out the truth."

"Wow…"

"Yeah. Good friend, right? But my dad was soon to learn the hard way that in this life you don't get something for nothing…" Jacob pauses. He stands up and paces the veranda, rubbing his forehead restlessly.

"As soon as university was over, Patrick moved into his first flat in London. He threw parties almost every weekend. He became obsessed with partying – he wanted booze, drugs and beautiful women. But he didn't have much luck with the ladies. Dad always said it was because he was too shit faced half the time to string a sentence together. Then one night… one night… oh for fuck's sake, I don't want you hearing this part," he snaps apprehensively.

"I'm sorry. But Elle said…"

"I know what Elle fucking said!" he snaps again, this time his voice sounding more like a growl. I don't think I have ever heard him this on edge before.

I wish Elle hadn't told me anything. I hate this. Jacob looks ready to punch a wall and I'm about ready to throw up. How much worse can this get?

CHAPTER EIGHTEEN

"One night, at a party, Patrick disappeared for a couple of hours, leaving my dad to host. When he finally came back, he had a young girl slumped against his shoulder. She looked barely eighteen. Patrick laughed and boasted to everyone about how he found her crying on a bench following an argument with her boyfriend. He chatted to her and invited her to his party but apparently she was hesitant, so he offered her some pill, so she'd relax. Next thing, she's being carried into his bedroom."

"Oh…"

"My dad was disgusted Mia. Disgusted. He got everyone to leave the party; he knew he needed to sort Patrick out and he didn't need a party going on whilst he did it. He got everyone to leave pretty quickly, but when he went to speak to Patrick, his bedroom door was locked and he had music blasting from his room. My dad tried to get in. He tried, but he couldn't. He didn't know what to do. He panicked. He left Patrick's and went back to his own flat. He was sick that night.

"At six o'clock the next morning, Patrick started ringing my dad constantly. When my dad finally answered, he said that Patrick was in tears. He was crying so hard he could barely catch his breath. My dad rushed to him and when he got there, Patrick blurted out that he had raped her."

My body shudders and my heart skips a beat at the word. Rape. That disgusting vile man who had his hands all over me raped someone. I know Elle said it, but hearing it come out of Jacob's mouth hits me differently.

I take a gulp of my water and a deep breath before reluctantly nodding to Jacob to continue telling me the story.

"Patrick just kept screaming at my dad to help him, repeatedly shouting that he owes him, he owes him. My dad wanted no part in what had happened, but things got ugly and Patrick threatened to tell my grandad everything. They argued for almost an hour and I guess in the end, Patrick wore my dad down and won, because together they hatched a plan.

"Patrick woke the girl up and told her to leave. Of course, she left confused, terrified, emotional and not in a good state. The first man she saw in the street when she got away from the flat would be my dad. My dad approached her and asked her if she was okay. She cried and told him that she believed she had just been raped. My dad showed her his card to prove he was a lawyer and promised to help her. He asked her to tell him exactly what had happened. Of course, the girl relayed everything as best she could and that was when my dad had the role of persuading her that she was at fault. He told her that there were no grounds for rape, that it sounded like she was drunk and had had consensual sex. He told her that she willingly went to his flat and willingly stayed the night. He told her she had no case. And the poor girl believed him."

"Okay. That's enough."

"No!" Jacob calls desperately as he stops me from walking away. "I'm not going to tell this story all over again Mia because each time I do it kills me. If you don't want to listen now you never will."

I sit back down.

"This is scaring me."

"Do I scare you?" Jacob asks so quietly I barely hear it.

I shake my head in response. "I don't think so."

"Then please Mia, trust that you know me. I don't like telling this story any more than you like hearing it. But after the thoughts that Elle put into your head about me, I need you to hear the truth." He's so vulnerable right now and I'm not used to it.

I lean back calmly in my seat and show him I'm listening.

"Patrick got off scot-free. Thanks to my dad scaring the girl to the point where I don't think she ever wanted to tell another soul," he states with sarcasm and disgust.

"Patrick was sorry for a very long time. He swore to my dad that it would never happen again. I think my dad believed him too, until he saw a new sleazy side to Patrick coming out. He'd always been sleazy to be fair, but this time he had a cockiness about him, no doubt because he had already got away with it once. My dad wanted to distance himself but at the same time he was scared about Patrick telling my family the truth. Every so often my grandad would search the house again for the heirloom and get himself all upset and into a state each time he couldn't find it. There was just no way my dad could admit to selling it. He genuinely thought it would kill my grandad. So, time went on and Patrick's secret was kept – begrudgingly. Unfortunately, years later is where I come into it."

"Okay. I'm ready to hear it." My lips press tightly together, either to stop me from changing my mind or from throwing up, I'm not sure which.

"One year, my parents threw their annual Christmas Eve party. It used to just be for the neighbours but over the years the invites grew and soon friends and work associates were all attending. One of the neighbours had a daughter called Deanna. She was only a year younger than me; she was very beautiful, funny, ditzy and not all that smart, but she was ambitious. I always had a bit of a thing for her when we were growing up, but of course, she wasn't smart enough or rich enough, so my parents deterred me from pursuing anything – after all, they had Elle in their sights. It didn't stop us from flirting excessively though. I think we both did it to annoy my mum really."

"What year did you say it was?"

"I was about twenty-four or twenty-five, so it would have been 2009, I guess. Why do you ask?"

"I was just curious as to how long you've been harbouring this," I softly say.

"It's not me who deserves your compassion," he replies, his head hanging down in shame.

"Maybe not but I still know a good man when I see one."

"Anyway," he sighs heavily. "That night Deanna and I got quite tipsy on our own in the garden whilst all the pompous rich folk drank my dad's best scotch and bitched about the recession and how it meant they'd probably have one less Barbados trip because of it that year, or some bullshit. Deanna ended up wasted – I think she was trying to keep up with me, but she couldn't handle it. She asked if she could have a lie down in my room. Of course I said yes, and I took her up there and allowed her to get comfortable in my bed. I knew she was drunk because she's usually pretty shy but before I had the chance to leave my room, she grabbed me by my shirt and asked me to have sex with her. Of course, I politely declined. I didn't want her feelings hurt but there was no way I was going to do anything with her, she wasn't in any state for it. To be fair, she didn't protest much. I had barely closed my bedroom door behind me when I heard her soft snores. I spent the rest of the night by myself in the games room where I must have fallen asleep, because the next thing I know, I'm waking up to screaming and shouting."

He stops to rub his head as if he wants to rub the memories away.

"Everyone had left the party, at least that's what my parents thought until they saw Patrick leaving my bedroom and zipping up his jeans with Deanna still passed out on my bed – the only difference was that she was naked now. She wasn't fucking naked when I left her there that's for damn sure. My mum freaked out, she was screaming, confused and scared. I got to them just in time to hear Patrick attempt to threaten my dad. 'Who will they believe?' he smugly questioned him. 'She's naked in Jacob's room, not mine,' he said with that awful smirk.

"Then of course he played his trump card. Either my dad had to fix his messes again or my grandad would learn some horrible truths. I don't know Mia, I really don't know why this heirloom has such a hold over my dad that he would lie like this, but all I know is that he looked at me in desperation to fix it. And I did."

"How?"

"I woke her up when it was just me and her again and I told her that she'd gotten herself naked and kept trying to have sex with me. Of course, she was embarrassed. She grabbed her clothes, apologised wholeheartedly and left. The next day, she came to my house to apologise again. I couldn't even look her in the eye. I'm a fucking scumbag for what I did. I let her believe that she should be embarrassed. I'm the one who is embarrassed. I'm embarrassed by where I come from, who I am and who my family is.

"Since that night I have avoided those parties and Patrick like the plague. Until Elle invited him to her party – and I knew full well she did it to get a little kick. She loves to mess with me, she always has. That's why I flew at him when I saw his hands all over you. I couldn't protect Deanna, but I knew I could protect you. And I'd do it again. I'd kill him if I had to. I'd kill him for you, Mia."

"Poor Deanna…" is all that manages to fall from my lips. "I'm sorry, I don't mean to add to your pain…"

"No, you're right. Poor Deanna, she's the only one who deserves your sympathy here. But I just need to know one thing: am I different to you now?"

CHAPTER NINETEEN

He needed a lot of my affection last night – it was like every touch gave him a tiny bit of reassurance. We talked some more. I cuddled into him each time, ran my fingers through his hair, stared into his eyes and reassured him as best I could that I'm not about to run away from him. I'm struggling to see how this makes Jacob a monster like Elle insinuated. It's quite possibly the most awful story I have ever heard. There are so many victims in it and it seems the only true winner is vile Patrick.

There is one thing I made clear to Jacob though – I told him that I wouldn't have any part in any dramas with Patrick and he promised me he wouldn't ever lie for anyone like that again. He kept telling me how much he hates himself and I believe him – it hurts me that he feels that way, but I understand.

No wonder he didn't want to have to tell that story ever again, it's not easy to digest and process. I'm still analysing everything now – every part of the story has me angry, devastated, feeling sick and helpless. It's horrific. Those poor girls. I even feel sorry for Jacob's dad – well, as much as I can feel sorry for a spineless twat.

Jacob sleeps soundly next to me, his beautiful lips softly pouted and his arm draped across my stomach. I wish I could have gone back to sleep as quickly as he did but it's hardly the best bedtime story I have ever heard. Whatever happened to a Hansel and Gretel? I'd have much preferred something like that.

The hotel telephone rings next to me, startling both me and Jacob.

"Hello?" I tiredly croak as I press the handset to my ear.

"I understand… I agree that would be the best thing to do… I'm sure I can work something out… Thank you, I'll speak with you soon," I answer every so often whilst Jacob watches me curiously.

"Who was that?" he asks as I place the phone back down.

"It was my mum's doctor," I say with a sad sigh. "We have come to the decision that it would be better to cremate her here. But it'll take up to a week for that to happen, so I told him I'd try to work something out and stay longer. Would that be okay with you? You can go back home to England if you want?"

"No way," he whispers gently as he takes hold of my hands and plants a soft kiss on them. "I'm here with you, to support you, no matter how long it takes. I'm going to be here for as long as you are."

"Thank you, I'm glad you're here."

"I'm glad too."

"I have to head down to the hospital and sign some forms for the cremation…"

"Give me a second to get ready and I'll come with you."

"It's okay, honestly, I won't be long. Take your time waking yourself up and then when I get back, I'll treat you to lunch – there's a little place nearby that serves the best cocktails," I say with a big smile as I recall my drunken antics there with Megan.

Jacob grabs me gently but passionately and pulls me in close before pressing his lips against mine.

"Can't wait," he says between kisses.

Of course, it would have been nice to take Jacob with me but after the intense conversation last night, a little break will do us both good. Plus, when it comes to my mum, I prefer to be on my own and be more private about it. I'm not sure if that's because I'm trying to be independent as usual or whether it's because a part of me still feels guilty about how I left things with her before she died and I have this horrible voice inside my head that tells me I'm a hypocrite for being upset about it now. I'm sure that it's just a symptom of grief – at least that's what I'm trying to tell myself.

The sunshine is beautifully bright and warm as always and I'm at the hospital in no time at all. I'm looking forward to getting back to the hotel already and spending some time with Jacob, and maybe even treating this as a holiday. It'll be the best distraction for me right now, even though this is not quite how I imagined my first trip abroad with Jacob would be. But as the saying goes: when life gives you lemons, make lemonade.

It's bittersweet seeing Dr Garcia again – he really is a nice man, it's just a shame that every time I see him, I remember him only for being the man to tell me my mum was dying. We spend some time discussing the cremation and he asks me if I have any ideas about where I would scatter her. I hadn't thought of it really, but now that he mentions it, it seems so fitting to scatter her in the ocean – after all, that's where she spent most of her life and where she was at her happiest.

"Have you got anyone to support you when the time comes to collect her ashes?" Dr Garcia asks me sweetly.

"I do, thank you, I have my partner, err, friend, partner-friend thing with me." Fuck. That caught me completely off guard. It feels weird to declare I'm with Jacob after all the hiding we had to do.

Dr Garcia arches one of his thick black bushy brows with confusion, before breaking into a smile as if I'm some schoolgirl who is admitting to her first crush.

"Great, well the address of where to go to collect your mother's ashes is in your paperwork. Be sure to take your partner-friend thing with you for support."

"Thank you," I giggle awkwardly. "And thank you again for all your support."

With that, I leave briskly. I'm eager to put the paperwork away in a drawer and try to relax my mind with a pina colada down by the swimming pool. I haven't been down to the pool yet, but it's huge and the aqua water is so inviting. It's a quiet hotel too, which I love – there's not too many guests or too much going on. It's a good place to re-energise.

I didn't pack any of my bikinis but I'm sure I can find something suitable in one of the lobby shops.

I'm back at the hotel within about fifteen minutes. I love stepping inside, the air-conditioning hits me every time and it is so refreshing. You can't walk around for too long outside, unless you don't mind being soaked through with sweat.

"Ms Johnson?" a vaguely familiar voice calls.

Oh bollocks, it's the poor young guy who I tried to flash my boobs at when I was drunk.

"Oh god! It's all just come flooding back," I gasp as my cheeks grow redder.
"I really must apologise. I've been going through some stuff and the mixture of alcohol and stress obviously doesn't agree with me. I'm so sorry for offering to show you my rack, and if I made you feel uncomfortable in any way."

"No, no, Ms Johnson, you are absolutely fine, I wasn't stopping you for an apology. My colleague said someone phoned with a message for you – he wrote it down and popped it into this envelope. I just wanted to make sure you got it."

"Ah, I see. Kind of wish you had interrupted me before I replayed the whole embarrassing scene," I say with a grin and he politely laughs.

"What scene? It's already forgotten about." He winks and suddenly the awkwardness has lifted, and we are just two people laughing about the crazy drunk British girl.

I take the envelope and begin opening it as I walk back to my room. I'll check on Jacob first and see if he wants to come to the lobby shops with me.

I open up the piece of card inside the envelope to read the message.

My darling Mia, don't forget your sunblock. The Bahamas gets awfully hot and I'd hate for you to burn. Love, Mum."

I reread it twice. A third time. Another time. It doesn't make sense. I spin back around on my heel and head back to reception.

"Excuse me, excuse me, Andrew?"

"Yes ma'am?"

"When did this call come in?"

"My colleague was doing the night shift and he said the call came through just before he clocked off, so I'm guessing around six-thirty this morning."

"Impossible," I mumble to myself as I feel my hands trembling. I run back to the room; I have to show Jacob.

I burst into the room with such a racket that Jacob jumps out of his seat.

"What's going on?" He rushes over to me, seeing how visibly shaken I am.

"Look… Look!" I shout, waving the note in his face.

I watch his eyes scan the note.

"Okay, calm down. I'm sure there's a reasonable explanation."

"Like what!?" I snap. "My mum is gone, she couldn't have possibly left this message, so who did? Because it is not cute or sweet. It's inappropriate."

"Maybe they misheard the name. Maybe it was Megan?"

"Megan and mum do not sound the same, Jacob."

"Maybe there's another Mia staying here and they got confused?"

"Or maybe someone is playing a horrible game with me."

"Who would do that sweetheart? Come on, you're stressing yourself out," Jacob says, trying his hardest to rationalise with me. He pulls me close and holds my body firmly against his.

"Does Elle know we're here?"

"In the Bahamas? Yeah, she does."

"You told her?"

"I told her I was coming to the Bahamas to be with you, yes. She knew you had left abruptly and she thought you were running away. I corrected her and told her that you needed to be by your mum's side."

"Great, so it's fucking Elle isn't it? Screwing with me."

"No, Mia, no. She's crazy yeah but not psychopath-kind of crazy."

"Are you defending her!?" I snap again, this time pushing him away from me.

"Fuck, NO! I wouldn't. But I am trying to calm you down and help you see that this is probably just a mistake. Come on baby, you didn't sleep well last night, things are getting on top of you."

I don't know anymore, maybe he's right. I haven't been sleeping well and I have been under probably more stress these past couple of months than ever before in my life.

"Mia, why don't you have a lie down? We can do the pool thing or eat later. I just want you to get some rest."

"Will you stay with me?" I ask, anxiously. I suddenly don't want to be alone anymore. This note has knocked me for six. I don't know what is going on and I can't think straight. But I do know I am sleep deprived and Jacob is right, a rest might help me.

"Of course, babe. I'll be lying right next to you the entire time."

CHAPTER TWENTY

"You seem a bit better now?" Jacob says, sounding as if he is trying to reassure himself more than me.

We have the swimming pool virtually to ourselves; I slept a lot longer than I thought I would so by the time we got ready and down to the pool it had already gone six o'clock, not that it matters. If anything, the timing couldn't have been more perfect – the sun is beginning to set behind the tall palm trees which creates a gorgeous orange glow against our skin.

"You know, the last time you and I were in water together you were very much misbehaving Ms Johnson, do you remember that?"

"Ah, the hot tub," I grin, my face screwed up at the awkward memory. I still can't believe that I have that side of me – it was like some small spark inside of me that I didn't know I had, not until I met someone who knew how to ignite it and before I knew it the spark turned into flames.

"It was fun, wasn't it?" But I don't need an answer, the hardening bulge in his swim shorts tells me that it was indeed fun.

Jacob sighs impatiently. I know that sigh – it's an 'I have to have you now' kind of sigh. "You certainly know how to get a man excited." He breathes deeply, his eyes staring suggestively down at me.

"Now?"

He nods before the biggest grin spreads across his full lips, showing the perfectly white teeth that I am always so jealous of.

"It's getting dark, we're the only ones down here now. I reckon if we just sneak over there behind that palm tree, nobody could see us."

I pull away from him, floating away on my back. He locks his eyes on me, waiting for the green light. Of course, I give him a smile and turn onto my front and swim over to the most secluded area, behind the large palm tree like Jacob suggested.

When I get there, I turn to face the edge of the pool and relax with my crossed arms in front of me on the tiles and allow my head to rest against them.

Within moments I feel Jacob's fingers slide down my back as he swims over and joins me.

"I love you," he softly whispers into my ear before grazing down and gently kissing and caressing my neck with the tip of his tongue which instantly brings heat in between my legs.

"Tell me you missed me," he says in a deep authoritative whisper.

I feel his hand take hold of the back of my bikini bottom and grasp it tightly within his palm, causing the fabric to stretch and mimic a thong.

"I've missed you," I gasp as he grips and pulls my bikini up further, forcing the fabric to rub harder against my butt crease, arousing me in ways I didn't know were possible until right now.

I have never considered anal and I have never even thought that it could be something I could enjoy, but right now, the way Jacob has me feeling, I want to feel him from behind. I want him to show me what I have been missing.

I feel myself panting already as I grip the side of the swimming pool and enjoy his touch. His hands grab either side of my hips and attempt to spin me around, but I push back against him, shaking my head.

"No," I whisper breathlessly. "I want it this way."

Jacob's breathing quickens in excitement. "You sure?" he asks but I'm already nodding.

"Okay. Let me get you ready for it."

I'm not sure what he means at first but he quickly pulls my bikini to the side and slowly inserts a finger into me. His finger penetrates me slowly to begin with but as I groan in anticipation, he picks up the pace before pushing in another finger.

"I'm ready, I want *you* now," I beg. I'm so horny and turned on that I can barely function. I'm not even scared of getting caught anymore. At this point, the entire hotel staff could come out and watch and I wouldn't give a shit. I'm putty, I am putty in Jacob's hands and he knows it.

Jacob's full length is pushed inside me and for a split second it stings, taking my breath away, but then it feels good, so good that I'm moaning uncontrollably. It's a different kind of pressure than I have ever felt before, it's rough, it's deep but it's sexy and I'm loving it.

Jacob's panting gets louder and joins in unison with mine. He brings his hand up to my wet hair and wraps it round his palm, pulling me back roughly. His demeanour is so commanding that with each thrust he makes me his. I will always be his.

The water becomes noticeably choppier as we come close to climaxing. I can feel Jacob tensing up behind me as his groans become deeper. My cheeks feel like they're burning, and I can feel myself throbbing with such vigorousness that the euphoria takes me close to the edge. I allow my fingers to find my most sensitive area and with a few strokes I spill over and both Jacob and I orgasm together.

My knees are so weak I can barely hold myself up in the water. I slow my breathing down before reconnecting with Jacob's gaze, who, apart from being exhausted too, looks completely smug. He knows exactly what he does to me, in the same way that I know what I do to him. Together it is electric, it is like nothing I have ever experienced before. He is like every romantic comedy I have ever watched and every erotic novel I have ever read. He is my perfect.

CHAPTER TWENTY-ONE

That evening I take Jacob to the Daiquiri Shack. It seems an odd comfort to go there after I spent the evening drowning my sorrows with my mum's best friend, Megan. But somehow, I feel closer to Mum being here. I'm not entirely sure if that makes any sense but I do.

I'm relieved when Jacob's eyes gaze around the little bar in amazement. All the fruits stacked up like a rainbow of treats look even more inviting than I remembered, and I can tell Jacob is as impressed as I was when I first stepped into this place.

I want to tell him more about what I learned from Megan, about my mum's mental health, and how she kept herself away to protect me. I want to tell him about the mysterious Cillian, the man she fell in love with. I have a lot more in common with my mum than I ever realised and I want to tell him that too, but I'm also aware that he is dealing with a lot himself – he has just left his wife and his family will soon be learning of his divorce. I don't want to put more on his plate than he needs. I can always tell him about her another time.

Our evening out makes me feel like we are on a care-free holiday. There is no mention of Elle and I choose to keep discussions of Mum to one side, so it's just us, living in the moment on this stunning island and it is heavenly to say the least. I make him try all my favourite cocktails first and then we dive into some new ones that we hadn't tried before, such as guava with sour orange. Okay, so you can quite possibly grab a carton of guava juice from your local supermarket, but clearly it is nowhere near as fresh or as amazing as this.

We end the evening with some extra hot chicken wings and a

coconut rum milkshake. It's a bit of an odd mix, and I'm not entirely sure how my stomach will cope with the mix of chilli and milk, but hey – when in Rome.

We take the slowest walk back to the hotel alongside the ocean. I kick my shoes off and carry them and allow my feet to sink into the warm sand with each step that I take. What is it about feeling the sand between your toes that feels so freeing? The world changes all the time – more modern, more technology, more buildings, but the one thing that remains the same is the ocean and I love the freedom and calmness that it brings. I'm starting to realise I sound like a hippy – I blame the island life.
I fight my deepest cringiest urges to draw our names surrounded by a love heart in the sand. It is perhaps one of the most clichéd things you can do on a beach – well that and having sex I guess.

Jacob slips his fingers into mine and it brings me so much comfort; it is definitely better than me scribbling our names into the sand. When we eventually get back to our hotel room, Jacob insists on running me a bath. I wait on the veranda like he asks me to and when I'm allowed into the bathroom, I see at least a dozen tealights surrounding the tub and a handful of rose petals floating on the soapy bubbly water.

"When you're ready to get out I'll be waiting on our bed with some lavender oil to rub into your shoulders."

"Lavender oil?"

"I got it from the lobby shops. You'd know there's some good stuff in there if you bothered to buy some clothes like I asked you to," he says with the most playful grin. Half of me wants to swat him away and protest at his cheeky statement while the other half wants to grab him and kiss him passionately. There's something about his smile that just makes me feel weak and so I give in and do the latter.

The bath is nice and hot, just how I like it. The heat engulfs my body and forces my muscles to relax. I hadn't realised how tense I had been until my body sinks deeper into the water. I keep lowering myself until my ears are under too and the water causes everything to become slightly muffled but mostly silent. It is so calming. I feel like I have managed to momentarily shut the world out, alongside any problems, and right now, nothing else matters.

Usually, I could quite happily relax in this bathtub for an hour but knowing Jacob is waiting for me next door is too tempting. I carefully climb out and wrap a soft white towel around my hair. I wipe the condensation from the mirror and see that my skin is a little pink from the hot water, but I do look refreshed and better than I did before.

I use another towel and dab it gently against my body before placing it back on the rail and tiptoeing naked into the bedroom to find Jacob gawping at me.

"It's too hot for a towel." I shrug nonchalantly but inside I'm trying my hardest not to giggle at Jacob's hungry eyes and open jaw.

Jacob's oily fingertips press firmly over my shoulder blades and across the back of my neck before gliding down my spine which gives me goosebumps. My body instantly relaxes underneath his warm hands.

"How's the pressure?"

"Hmm-hmm," I mumble, sleepily.

His thumbs begin making circular motions in the small of my back, relieving pressure I didn't even know I had.

"I love your body," I hear Jacob whisper under his breath. I pretend I didn't hear, although the subtle smile on my face may indicate otherwise.

I love feeling his big hands gliding up my back, rubbing my shoulders and then gliding back down to my lower back. I feel a few extra drops of lavender oil being carefully drizzled onto my skin. His hands firmly rub the oil into me in a way that makes me grow a little aroused.

The thought of my moist skin against his is an image I can't ignore.

I carefully manoeuvre myself between his legs until I'm free enough to turn on my back, revealing my naked body, still slightly damp from my hot bath.
Jacob's eyes immediately flicker up and down my body, staring intently at every inch of me.

His expression suddenly changes to concern. "This isn't why I did this. I love sex with you, Mia. But I just wanted to relax you. I just want to look after you."

"I know that." His eyes darken as I lick my lips. "But I want you. I want to feel you."

I have never felt this way about anyone before, but with Jacob it's more than sex. I feel safe when his body is wrapped around mine; I feel wanted, needed; I feel like he absorbs every part of me.

"Say it then." His voice deepens as the hunger grows in his voice.

"I want you."

"More..." Jacob whispers as he wraps one of my legs around his waist and lowers onto me.

"I need you," I manage to mumble just as I feel his hard length thrust inside of me.

"Forever?"

"Forever," I promise as he deepens inside of me with another thrust, making me catch my breath.

Jacob grabs the lavender oil beside him and trickles it over my breasts and down to my navel, causing my body to arch.

I snatch the bottle before he has a chance to put it back down and smile as I return the favour, smothering his torso in oil which highlights every muscle and every dent of his chiselled body.

This time our sex is different, it's more sensual than it has been before. Jacob hungrily kisses me as if he needs to taste me, and our oily bodies rub easily and freely over each other, adding to the intensity of our passion. Jacob's hands find my wrists and he pins them beside my head and takes full control of me.
I bite down hard on his bottom lip between kisses which makes him groan. I love hearing that noise, especially as I know I'm the one causing it.

I wriggle one wrist free and grip it through his hair instead, holding him close to my face; his free hand scoops underneath my back and clutches me tightly. The safe feeling is back. Nothing matters right now, just me, with Jacob. Enjoying every inch of him, just as he is with me.

* * *

I'm awoken from my deep sleep by the subtle sound of my phone vibrating against the side table. I grab it quickly so that it doesn't disturb Jacob who is sleeping peacefully next to me. It's an unknown number. I wrack my brains trying to think who could be calling me at this time of night. Then again, I'm in the Bahamas – it's not that late back home. I answer it and hold the phone against my ear as I quickly walk out onto the veranda to avoid Jacob hearing.

The call is muffled, almost crackly, and I can barely hear anything clearly.

"Hello? Hello?"

I hear faint laughing. But not a genuine, happy laugh – it sounds more sadistic, creepy.

"Hello?" I ask again anxiously.

The laughing grows louder – it's a haunting noise, and the hairs stand up on the back of my neck. Something feels off.

"I'm hanging up!" I threaten.

"WHY DID YOU LET MUMMY DIE?!" the voice screeches into the phone before the line goes dead and I drop my phone in sheer panic.

I fight to slow my breathing, but my heart is slamming against my chest and my ears are ringing from that screeching. My hands are trembling and clammy.

"Jacob!" I scream. "Jacob!"

CHAPTER TWENTY-TWO

The day is spent with Jacob pacing our room and making phone call after phone call. He now agrees that my weird middle-of-the-night phone call, along with the message left at reception, seem quite sinister. The only problem is, he is convinced it is Alex doing this. He has been ringing around his contacts all morning and eventually he got in touch with an old colleague who is now a private detective.

"I don't care what the costs are, just find me evidence of that scumbag stalking my girlfriend and I'll write you any cheque you want," is a sentence that I have heard a few times now.

"I really don't think this is Alex," I say as soon as Jacob hangs up the phone.

"Who else would it be?"

"I don't know yet. But it won't be him. He doesn't know that my mum has passed away or even that she was ill. He doesn't know I'm here and above all else, the voice was female!" I throw my arms up in the air as if I have made enough valid points.

Jacob's stare changes and I think he realises that I must be right.

"Could it be another jealous ex-lover of yours?"

I frown instantly – how many people does he think I have been with?

"I suppose it could be Mr Patel at number eight, but then again the sex was awkward, what with his Zimmer-frame getting in the way. We gave up in the end so I'm sure he won't be missing that. Plus, he's deaf and eighty-six years old, so I'm not too sure he has the tools to pull this off," I trail off as Jacob sighs impatiently, clearly unimpressed with my sarcasm.

"I just meant..." he takes a step forward and lowers his tone as if he is about to share a secret, "well, have there been any more desperate guys following you home from the bar, like that other prick?"

I gulp hard as I try to keep myself from losing my composure. "Desperate?"

"I didn't mean you. I meant them. They're the ones desperate for a shag, Mia. Come on don't twist my words."

"How does that make it ANY better?" I snap, growing agitated.

"Well I don't know what you got up to before me, do I? You're hardly shy, Mia."

"Excuse me?"

"I just meant... Look, you're beautiful, guys look at you. I'm just saying, I'm sure there must have been other guys."

I take a step back; it would be much safer for him if there was distance between us right now.

"You know, I thought lawyers were supposed to be good with words, and yet what you just said couldn't have been any worse," I say, grabbing my bag and heading for the door.

"Wait!" Jacob calls and I feel him lunge towards me and grab me by my arm.

I turn so my back is against the door and notice the sad look of desperation in Jacob's eyes.

"I didn't mean what I said, it's just, there's a lot of shit on my mind and I just want to protect you." My heart lurches at Jacob trying to protect me. Shame he has a shitty way of expressing himself.

"I'm still going for a walk," I say as I shrug him off my arm. "But don't worry, I'll try not to bring any desperate blokes back with me."

I don't even give him the chance to respond as I shut the door quickly and power walk down towards the lobby.

"Ms Johnson?" I'm waved over by a short woman at reception; standing next to her is Andrew who must have told her who I am because I haven't seen this particular woman at reception before.

"Yes?" I respond, feeling stressed out and confused. Has Jacob been on the phone already, asking them to stop me from leaving whilst he comes down to dig an even bigger hole?

"We have a note for you. Well actually, it was an email sent to us, but we printed it off for you. If you don't mind me saying Ms Johnson, I'm not sure whether it's a practical joke or something more serious, but we can call the police for you if you think you are being harassed?"

The woman looks worried as she hands me the folded-up piece of paper, which causes the little hairs on the back of my neck to stand up and a chill to race down my spine.

I'm not sure how to respond, so I don't. I awkwardly smile and nod, taking small steps backwards until I'm closer to the exit. As soon as I'm out of the hotel, I quickly unfold the piece of paper. What can it be this time?

From: Anonymousfun@gmail.com
To: OceanClubHtl@aol.com

Subject – FAO MIA JOHNSON

ROSES ARE RED,
VIOLETS ARE BLUE,
YOUR MUM WAS A WHORE
AND SO ARE YOU.

I'm not sure what is worse – the horrible insult to my dead mother or the fact that the email address is clearly one that has just been made up and therefore I'm still none the wiser as to who is doing this. A different emotion sparks through me this time – not just fear, but anger too. How dare they speak about my mum like this? Who would say such things? She's barely cold – how could someone be so fucking cruel?

I'm angry and I don't feel like I have anywhere to go right now. I can't go back and sit with Jacob and anyway, I'm not in the mood to be stuck in the hotel room. I need a large vodka and I need it now.

I have the Daiquiri Shack in mind, but I find a small blues bar much closer. It's tiny and smells a bit stale but it has vodka and, with the mood I'm in, I'm not picky.

I sit on an old wooden bar stool tucked away in the corner and order my tipple.

What if it is Alex? He had my mum's phone number, maybe he phoned her and someone at the hospital answered and told him what had happened. Maybe he said he was my husband and they gave him all the information he needed. Maybe he phoned around all the hotels on this island until he found me. My brain races and races a million miles an hour, different thoughts popping in and out of my brain so quickly that it leaves my head feeling fuzzy. I knock back a shot of vodka and welcome the burn against my throat.

"Another two please," I say to the server as the air leaves my lungs.

CHAPTER TWENTY-THREE

"Ma'am, I think other people were hoping to do some karaoke this evening," the dark shaggy-haired barman says as he reaches out to grab the microphone, but I snatch it away before he has the chance.

"Not a chance! I can't let my fans down," I announce proudly as I lift my glass up to toast the eight elderly customers who are watching me in dismay and confusion.

"Okay, so we've had Celine Dion, 'All by Myself', we've had Sister Sledge, we've had Abba, what shall we sing next? Ah yes! This one is for my stalker!"

I'm fully aware that the small crowd of people are practically gawping at me as if I am having some kind of public mental breakdown, but thanks to the vodka, I couldn't care even if I wanted to, plus I can barely see their faces anyway, they've become blurs thanks to the vodkas I've been downing. Just blurs spinning slowly around the room.

I clear my throat dramatically as 'Somebody's Watching Me' by Rockwell begins to play through the speakers.

"Here we go!" I shout overexcitedly. "I always feel like somebody's watching me…" – I switch my voice up to a high-pitched scream for reasons unknown to me – "AND I HAVE NO PRIVACY! Whoop whoop! Sing it bitches!"

The bar remains silent. It's always awkward when a crowd refuses to join in.

I am now doing what can only be described as a mum dance – you know, the kind of dance your mum probably did back in the seventies. I take a few steps to the left and then kick, then back to the right and kick. No idea what the fuck I'm doing, but I throw one of my arms in the air for good measure.

"Another chorus, come on, everybody this time!"

I swing my arm side to side in the air as if I'm in some boyband performing in London's Wembley Arena; of course, nobody joins in, but God loves a trier and tonight I'm Beyoncé. Actually, my hair is crazy and sweaty and sticking up all over the place, and I probably look more like Meat Loaf, but the vodka gives me the confidence to believe otherwise.
"I ALWAYS feel like, Somebody's WATCHING ME, WHO'S PLAY-ING TRICKS ON ME?" I trail off as in the corner of my eye I sud-denly spot a sweaty-looking Jacob appear in the doorway.

Oh fuck.

He is wearing a tight white t-shirt covered in sweat, at least I think it's sweat. His hair, which is normally well styled, is all dishevelled and flopped to one side.

"Bahamas you've been fantastic. But I think my taxi is here," I say with a semi-grin on my face, hoping to make Jacob laugh, but his face is as serious as Dr Garcia's when he told me my mum was dying. Tragic.

Jacob begins impatiently pushing through the crowd of people gathered around the stage worshipping me. Of course, that's bullshit – in reality, he is politely manoeuvring through the eld-erly onlookers.

"Oh my god. Are we about to have an *Officer and a Gentleman* mo-ment? I fucking love that movie," I giggle into the microphone as an unimpressed Jacob keeps his eyes locked onto mine.

"Shit, he is totally going to carry me out of here like in that scene!" I drop the microphone to the floor and prepare for my ro-mantic but flamboyant exit.

Jacob roughly grabs me by the legs and swings me in a most unladylike way over his shoulder in what can only be described as a fucking fireman's carry.

"Jacob!" I squeal as I try to wriggle free. "I'm not a fucking farm animal, put me down!"

Of course, Jacob ignores me and continues dragging my drunken arse out of the bar before eventually flopping me down onto the pavement outside causing my legs to buckle beneath me and leaving me sitting on the floor.

"Well, thanks very fucking much Jacob. You totally killed my vibe, but whatever."

"Have you any idea what fucking time it is, Mia?" Jacob growls as his hands fly around dramatically. He isn't really one for speaking with his hands – until he is this angry, then I guess he changes his mind.

"No, *Dad*, I'm so sorry, I must have lost track, what *is* the time?"

"Don't start this shit with me Mia, I'm not in the fucking mood. Do you have *any* idea how fucking worried I have been?"

"I'm a big girl."

"Yeah, a big girl who is going through a lot of shit. You've just lost your mum, your fucking ex-husband recently hurt you, you're out here drinking alone and now you have some stalker. So, can you imagine what I have been thinking, pacing in that fucking hotel room on my own?" The pain in his voice is evident and instantly changes my mood. My giggling has stopped and instead a tear stings my eye.

"I miss her," I manage to mumble just before my eyes swell and tears seamlessly fall down my cheeks. My bottom lip quivers uncontrollably and I look up at Jacob, who automatically softens his demeanour.

"Life is just so fucking short, you know. You never know when your time is up. We all live life like we assume people will be there forever. We argue over petty stuff like we can make up with that person anytime we want because we've got a whole lifetime left, but that's just not true is it? The last time I spoke with my mum I was arguing with her. Had I known that… you know… well, I wouldn't have ended it that way…"

Jacob crouches down to get closer to my level and studies my face sympathetically. He brings his warm hand up to my face and gently wipes my tears away with his thumb. I suddenly feel so exposed and silly. Moments ago, I was performing my world tour on stage and now I'm sprawled out on this pavement crying like a child. I wriggle free from his hand and attempt to change the subject.

"I got another note," I croak as I fish the piece of paper out of my bag.

"*Another!?*"

I nod and hand him the crumpled paper. He furiously opens it up, knowing already that it's going to be disturbing.

His eyes scan back and forth across the paper as he reads the words. His eyes darken with anger and his jaw drops in shock.

"I'll kill him!" he hisses through gritted teeth.

"Who?"

"Alex! Who else?"

I'm too drunk to argue. Maybe it is Alex after all. He *did* hurt me, he threatened me, maybe he has progressed to stalking. Who knows anymore?

"I'm sorry for arguing with you. I'm sorry for the shit I said, I didn't mean for it to come out the way it did. It's just, this is probably the most on edge I have ever been. Somebody is threatening the person I love. I don't know how to deal with that." Jacob speaks so softly and I forgive him instantly. I can see the concern in his eyes, and I love him for it.

"I just want us to be a team and not go against each other over this," I say.

"And we will be. Just as long as you don't keep disappearing on me to badly sing karaoke to terrified locals," he teases with a big cheesy grin and I flop my head into his neck, giggling but dozing as the vodka washes me with tiredness. "Come on DJ Drunkmess, let's get you to bed."

CHAPTER TWENTY-FOUR

In hindsight, those vodkas probably weren't a good idea last night. I don't even remember getting into bed. My last memory is of me sitting on the pavement outside the bar sobbing about missing my mum and telling Jacob that I received another note. After that is anyone's guess. Jacob said I tried to seduce him when we got back to the room – I bet that was attractive in my drunken state! Thank god I wasn't puking again, or I might have scarred him for life.

I woke up half naked, mascara smudged around my eyes and in perfect streaks to show I'd been crying; I had lipstick smudged down my chin and one of my lash strips was on my forehead. I don't even remember putting that much make-up on.

It's about time I got my shit together. I had thought that staying in the Bahamas would give me time to grieve and refresh before I head back home but in reality, I've got too much spare time on my hands and I'm finding myself overthinking every little thing. I just want to dive back into my job and keep myself as busy with work as I can.

Thankfully, I don't have much longer here. Dr Garcia woke me up early this morning with a phone call to say that Mum's ashes would be ready to collect later today. He didn't have to ring me personally, but he has been so helpful and supportive whilst I have been here. The call prompted Jacob to sort us out some flights home – so hopefully tomorrow evening we will leave here. I say hopefully, but it is obviously bittersweet. I'm eager to get home and get back into my routine in the hope that it'll make me feel better, but this island has made me feel the closest to my mum I have felt in a long time, and I will miss this beautiful place.

Jacob holds my hand tightly in the taxi all the way to the small chapel of rest next to the hospital and every time I catch his eye, he offers me a small sympathetic smile. I'm grateful that I'm not on my own today. I'm already hungover and emotional, and I'm not sure how I'd have coped without him. I probably would have ended up with another panic attack, but with Jacob's hand in mine I feel calmer.

I'm not allowing myself to think of the new note I got last night. I won't have whoever is doing it win, especially not today. Today is about saying my very final goodbye to my mum, and this stalker won't ruin that for me.

I text Megan on the way and ask her if she is around to join me in scattering Mum's ashes. I would love for her to be there too, but unfortunately she sends me a quick message back to let me know she has just docked in Florida and won't be back in the Bahamas for another ten days. It's a shame, but her text reminds me of messages I'd get from my mum – she was always flitting between Florida and the Caribbean – and it makes me smile recalling that.

Another text comes through from Megan just as we reach the chapel.

'Go to Cove Bay for her ashes, I promise you, you won't regret it! It was one of your mum's most favourite places.'

I lean across to Jacob and show him the text message; he smiles and nods his head before getting his phone out of his pocket and looking up the place on Google.

On the outside, the chapel is beautiful – it is pristinely clean, and almost looks brand new. The creamy coloured building is bright against the blue skies and I feel some comfort that this picturesque chapel is where my mum has been resting until I could come and collect her.

We are greeted by an elderly gentleman dressed in a smart black suit and crisp white shirt with his sparse hair combed back covering his bald patch. The effort that he has made to look smart is adorable and his kind smile makes me melt. What a gentleman. Jacob can sense I'm feeling quite nervous though, so he takes the lead so that I don't have to.

After a short back and forth conversation, the man briefly disappears and when he returns, he holds an iridescent pearl-coloured urn in his hands.

"I hope you don't mind, but I've been telling your mother all about the time I saw Frank Sinatra performing in New York back in 1979 – probably one of the biggest highlights of my life," he tells us proudly.

"Ah, she's always been a great listener." I attempt a joke to lighten the atmosphere a little. I can already feel the anxiety rising from the pit of my stomach after seeing the urn – knowing my mum is inside it is a lot to bear.

He responds brightly and offers a smile as if he appreciates my good humour. You can tell he is a kind man and the more he talks, I realise he is from New York himself – his accent isn't as thick, but you can tell it used to be.

"I have some paperwork for you to sign before you can leave with her. Would you like a cup of caw-fee whilst you wait?"

Caw-fee. Brilliant. That's how coffee should always be pronounced.

"No thank you, even though you said it so brilliantly!"

He puffs up his chest proudly.

"You like the accent, huh?"

"I love it! I visited New York once before and I'd love to go again, especially at Christmas time."

"New York is the best city in the world! Leave your e-mail address on the form and I'll send over some real hidden gems in the city that you'll love. You like music, right?"

"Absolutely!" I beam, delighted to have a normal conversation.

"Great! I know all the hot spots and best joints. I know a little bar that Frank Sinatra used to attend after his concerts to unwind. He's from New Jersey you know?"

"No, I didn't know that. That's awesome. I'd love to see it for myself."

"Well, perhaps your husband can take you one day!" the kind man jokes and jests with Jacob who can't help but smirk.

I get the feeling this sweet old man could talk about Frank Sinatra and New York all day and to be honest I could happily listen. I love when people have a story to tell that they are passionate about. But we need to keep moving, so I sign the papers quickly and we exchange some typical pleasantries before he hands me the urn and waves us off.

It's a surreal feeling walking back outside with an urn filled with my mum's ashes. I'm not sure what the correct way to feel is, but I feel physically sick. I can hear the ashes swooshing against the urn as I tiptoe carefully down the steps and back towards the taxi.

"Do you want me to hold it? I mean her?" Jacob stumbles over his words, looking dejected as he panics, thinking he may have fucked up.

I smile reassuringly. There's hardly a manual on the correct way to speak when discussing someone's ashes. I'm not so sensitive that I'll jump down his throat for his choice of words.

Jacob takes a deep breath and changes his expression to a lighter one.

"Good news is that I found the cove Megan suggested. It's about thirty-five minutes from here."

"Oh, is that okay? Will that not be really expensive?"

Jacob takes hold of one of my hands and holds it tightly against his stomach, forcing me to hold the urn with just one hand which I nervously press against my chest.

"Don't be silly. I don't ever want you to worry about money. It's noble of you, but relax. I got this."

CHAPTER TWENTY-FIVE

As we approach the final ten minutes of the car journey, I realise our surroundings are becoming more and more rural. It's been a while now since I saw a hotel, or a resort or even a bar of some kind. In the last few minutes, the road has become more of a bumpy dirt track and the only thing I can see around us are palm trees with broken coconuts on the ground next to them. It seems like a fairly unvisited area of the island which brings me a sense of calm. I'm grateful to Megan for telling us about this place – I have a really positive feeling about it.

Jacob looks out of the car window in amazement. It's like we are driving into our own private slice of paradise. I clutch Mum tightly against my chest; I'm not saying any words out loud, but I'm talking to her inside my head. I'm comforting her. I'm telling her that she is about to be free and at peace. I tell her that I'm scared to let her go but I know it's what she would have wanted. And it may be childish or crazy, but I'm pretending that she is talking back. I pretend that she is giving me her approval on Jacob and smiling as she sees him reaching out to rest his hand on my knee; I pretend she smiles as he comforts me and she breathes a sigh of relief that although she's leaving, she knows I am in safe hands. I imagine we are having this little private moment where we kind of let each other know that everything is going to be okay and that I can let her go now.

Suddenly, the car journey comes to an abrupt end and it appears we have reached our destination. The taxi driver informs us it's not safe for him to go any further by car because of the steep cliff side and tells us where we can walk instead.

Jacob gives him some extra cash and asks him to wait for us to return; he nods, unphased, and gestures towards a footpath.

Like the gentleman he is, Jacob opens my car door and helps me out with Mum's urn still safely tucked beneath my arm.

"Holy sh…" Jacob sighs under his breath, prompting me to look in his direction.

Wow. No wonder this was a favourite spot of Mum's.

The ocean looks crystal clear, it is the bluest I have seen the water on this island, and the white waves complement it like dustings of glitter that sparkle under the sunshine. Trailing out into the ocean is a large broken rock that is shaped like an arch, adding to its magnificence.

It is the most unspoiled, untouched, beautiful spot I have ever seen. It is breath-taking. Jacob turns back to look at me, his smile spread from ear to ear showing those perfectly white teeth that I love so much.

"This is perfect for your mum," he says so happily; he is delighted for me.

Jacob carefully helps me down onto the narrow footpath. It's mixed with sand and rocks which makes it quite uneven to walk on, but Jacob steadies me with every step and eventually we make it safely onto the small beach.

I kick my shoes off and leave them by the footpath; the sand is pretty hot and burns my soles slightly but it's not off-putting. I enjoy feeling the warmth on my feet. Jacob politely follows my lead and removes his shoes too. He didn't have to, but the thought is appreciated.

"Where shall we go?" he asks.

"Definitely close to the arch – that way, I'll always know the exact spot we scattered her, if we ever come back."

Jacob drops his head down to try and hide his smile from me, but I see it too easily.

I smirk at his feeble attempt to hide his face.

"What's with the smile?"

He shrugs awkwardly before bringing up his head and showing his gorgeous smile again.

"You said *we* that's all. I love that."

"Well of course! But don't forget you owe me a New York trip too." I nudge him playfully.

"I knew that guy was going to cost me another holiday."

"Well, it would be criminal not to see Frank Sinatra's favourite bar."

"Since when did you become such a fan of Frank Sinatra?"

"What are you talking about? I have been a huge fan of Frank Sinatra for ages. At least a full hour now." I wink and giggle as he wraps his arm around my waist and plants a kiss on my forehead.

"The best is yet to come," he whispers into my ear. "And since you're Frank's biggest fan, you'll know that I just quoted one of his most famous songs."

"Of course I knew…" I try to say confidently but really, I had no clue and he knows it.

Our feet sink into the deep warm sand as we make our way towards the arch. It feels strange to know that I'm about to scatter my mum and end this chapter of my life.

"Would you like to say something?" Jacob asks.

"I'm not sure," I answer. "It just seems cheesy. I know it's not. But it just feels silly to talk out loud about how I feel when I know she can't hear me anymore."

"Who says she can't?"

I roll my eyes desperately. "Oh come on Jacob, we aren't religious."

"Who says you have to be religious to believe?"

"You know what I mean…"

"Say something. What's the worst that can happen? You won't regret it, that much I know."

I shrug awkwardly as I stand in the exact spot I want to scatter her. I have never been great with sharing feelings.

"Tina Anderson…" Jacob surprises me by speaking up, his hands crossed in front of his body mimicking a real memorial. "It seems a real shame that I didn't get to meet you, because if you have any resemblance to your daughter, then I know you were beautiful, charismatic, funny and kind. You're going now, far too soon for our liking, but if there is anything I can promise to make your last moments with us any easier, it is that I promise to take care of your daughter, whom I love."

"Whom?"

"Despite the fact she's occasionally a dickhead," he adds and I burst out laughing.

"Okay, okay, she would have liked that!"

"Good. Because it's your turn now…"

My eyes flicker anxiously from the urn in my hands to the sand, to the sea and back again. I hate being put on the spot. I hate goodbyes even more.

"Finally, you're with Dad now and you can't disappear on a cruise…" I mumble timidly.

Jacob's eyebrow arches at me as if to suggest I should stop using humour to hide behind and get on with it.

"The last few days I have had a lot of time to think and reflect on everything and I have so many regrets which hurt me because I can't fix them now. At least not with you. But if there is anything I want you to know before I lay you to rest, it's that I love you. I love you very much Mum and I am sorry if I ever made you feel like I didn't." My throat pinches a little as the emotions begin to stir inside of me.

Jacob nods at me like I'm doing brilliantly, and it gives me the courage to continue.

"I gave you a hard time sometimes, but it was only because I missed you when you were working away. The truth is, I couldn't have asked for a better mum. Especially one who rocks up to the school run in Ray-bans and a red lippie, like the rockstar you are." Jacob smiles at the thought.

"And as for Jacob, you'd love him. I'm really happy now Mum and I hope you are too, wherever you may be. Rest easy."

I wipe a tear from the corner of my eye.

"That's all I can say right now," I croak as I hide my tears from Jacob.

"It was more than enough. It was beautiful."

Jacob reaches down and takes hold of the urn. I carefully remove the lid and brace myself for a split second before I look at the ashes visible to me now.

I gulp hard and push away the tears. Jacob notices my fight to stay composed and strokes my hand with his thumb as I still hold on to the lid.

"Ready?" he asks gently and I nod.

We take a few steps into the warm water and stop just as it begins gently lapping against our shins.

Just as I angle the urn to spread Mum's ashes, a gentle breeze comes along and carries her a little way over the ocean before she rains down lightly onto the waves. It is actually pretty perfect.

CHAPTER TWENTY-SIX

I offered to pay for my own plane ticket home, but Jacob insisted he had it.

I think he's caught the travel bug because at the airport all he could think about was planning another trip. We discussed New York, Canada, New Zealand, a huge array of places. I felt excited thinking about our future plans. I couldn't think of anyone better to see the world with.

"Are you okay?" he asked a couple of hours into the flight. "You look bored."

"I am bored," I laugh. "It is a nine-hour flight after all."

"Why don't you put on a movie or *The Big Bang Theory*?"

"Nah, I struggle to pay attention to stuff when I'm on a plane. I'd rather just stare out of the window and enjoy the clouds."

"Well, I have something that'll make you smile."

"Oh, we're joining the mile-high club are we?"

Jacob screws his face up at me. "No, not that you pervert!"

Jacob reaches down for his small carry-on bag and fishes around for something. I sit upright, eager to see.

"Here." He smiles as he presents me with a square package wrapped in lilac tissue paper. "I was going to give it to you when we got back home, but we have six hours left of this flight and I'd like to see at least one smile."

I carefully fold back the paper and instantly I see his beautiful smile. It's us. Grinning from ear to ear in our first selfie, taken down on the beach the night after the Daiquiri Shack, in a sweet little golden frame. We look so happy together. We look good together – his bright white smile and floppy dark hair complements my peachy skin and blonde waves. I'm glowing next to him.

"I absolutely love it."

"I noticed when I was in your house that apart from the photo of you and your dad, you don't have that many. So, I wanted to change that." He says it so sweetly that I feel butterflies in my stomach and an electricity running through me that makes me feel so alive.

"I can't wait to hang this up. It'll go somewhere special, I promise." I nestle my head into Jacob's shoulder and keep the frame on my lap. He turns his head and kisses the top of my forehead; I inhale his cologne and rest my eyes, soaking up this moment.

The remainder of the flight is fairly uneventful. Jacob watches the tv show *Friends* and laughs along which I love. I sip cups of tea and watch as the sun
slowly rises over England.

By the time we are out of the airport, it's well past lunchtime. It took forever to get through security and even longer to get our luggage. Seems our bags were the very last ones thrown onto the belt.

On the car ride home Jacob discusses his plans with me. He tells me he'll let Elle stay in the house for as long as she needs, and he'll rent an apartment in town temporarily.

"What if Elle never wants to leave the house?"

"Then it's hers. It's just bricks and mortar. It's the sort of shit that matters to her but not me. If it means that much, she can have it."

"And? We just become neighbours with your ex-wife? That's not awkward at all."

I stare at him as if he has lost his marbles somewhere over the Atlantic.

"Well, I hadn't planned that far. I guess I thought if that was the situation you'd sell up and we would find somewhere fresh together."

"But I love my glass house," I whine. "It's bright and beautiful and mine."

The car ride becomes silent. I guess there are a lot of things we have yet to discuss and a lot of unanswered questions.

As we pull into our cul-de-sac, the atmosphere takes yet another shift.

"Fuck," Jacob breathes heavily as I pull into my driveway.

I look quickly in my rear mirror but don't see anything out of the ordinary.

"What?"

"The car on the drive…"

"Oh? Whose is it?" I ask, concerned. The face Jacob is pulling suggests it isn't good.

"That's my parents' car," he puffs agitatedly.

"Par-ents?" I repeat but I heard him clearly the first time.

"What is she playing at?"

"Shall I call you later?" I ask. I'm not really sure what I'm supposed to do. I want to be supportive, but I don't want him to think he has to worry about me.

"No way. If she wants to pull some stupid stunt, then it's the perfect time for me to introduce you. That way, there's no confusion or mix-ups. I'm with you now, I love you and that's the way it is."

"Woah, let's just take a moment. I don't want to ambush your parents here. We just got off an overnight flight, and I look awful – they'll probably think you're having a mid-life crisis being with me!" I try to sound reasonable but it's coming out like a hysterical screech.

"I thought we were a team?" He makes a frustratingly good point.

"We are, of course we are, but I don't want to get in the way of you and your parents."

"Mia, when I go in there, I want you by my side. Do I have to beg?"

I roll my eyes in angst. "No, of course you don't."

Jacob takes the lead up to the house, his strides long and charged, as if he is ready to fight.

I, on the other hand, am falling behind, timidly following and terrified about what is on the other side of the door.

What a welcome home this is! I'd been planning on a hot bubble bath and an early night but instead I'm about to come face to face with Elle *again* and meet Jacob's parents for the first time.

Fuck, my anxiety has crept on and is making me feel nauseous. I don't usually suffer from stomach problems, well not since I was a teenager, but right now my stomach is flipping, and I feel horrendous.

Whatever happens in there, I will defend Jacob. I will take all the blame and plead with his parents not to take it out on him. I will assure them that I can make him happy and that this isn't some silly little crush. I will make them like me. I don't know how, after all they are going to see me as a homewrecker, but I will try my hardest.

Oh god, I'm feeling really nauseous. I breathe deeply in through my nose and exhale slowly out of my mouth. Please don't be sick, please don't be sick.

CHAPTER TWENTY-SEVEN

Jacob steps inside first and I follow closely behind. The first thing I notice is that the house smells of homemade cooking, like a roast dinner or something similar. I imagine Elle has been whipping up a storm like some domestic goddess for the sake of Jacob's parents and they're probably all sitting around the main table now, tucking into their expensive lamb shanks and sipping a fine wine. There's the faint muffled noise of people talking in hushed tones coming from the kitchen.

Jacob takes me by the hand and leads us into the kitchen. He has an authoritative approach; I, however, am ready to run out of this place like Usain Bolt.

"Ah, here they are! The happy couple," Elle squawks unkindly as she knocks back her glass of red wine. "We didn't actually expect you home so soon – we thought you were honeymooning."

"Don't be ridiculous, Elle. I told you I was supporting Mia; her mother was very unwell."

"Ah yes, what was her name again? Something working class like… Terri?"

She shoots me a glare and a huge smirk spreads across her red lips as if she is waiting for me to defuse the bomb she's thrown at me.

"Tina," I correct her, desperately trying to keep my composure.

I realise that I'm being stared at. In the background, I see two faces at the dining table looking me up and down, but I avoid eye contact. My heart quickens and my cheeks flush red; it feels like a hundred degrees in here.

The blurry face to the left of me begins to stand up and I realise it is Jacob's father.

"Son, what the hell has happened here? Your mum and I are so disappointed," his husky voice announces like a stab wound to the chest. I can't imagine how Jacob feels.

I leave my head hung in shame as if I have guilt written all over it that I need to hide.

Jacob's jaw clenches whilst he thinks about his next move. But I think the word disappointed is blurring his vision.

"Choosing to make myself happy makes you disappointed does it, Dad?" he eventually asks, looking hurt and angry in one.

"Son, we worked so hard for this life and you've thrown it away like it means nothing."

"No Dad, *you* worked so hard for this life. I wasn't given much of a choice."

My eyes dart between them like I'm watching an intense tennis match at Wimbledon.

"We did what we thought would be the best for you and *this* family!"

"But it's not about me is it? It's about what looks good for this family, it always has been."

Jacob's mum rises to her feet, folds her arms and readies herself to weigh in.
"Well, maybe it has, but I can hardly introduce this... woman at our annual parties, can I? I mean, what is she? Some hairdresser from Essex?"

Elle nearly chokes on her fresh glass of red wine as she snorts with laughter at this stereotyping of me.

"No! But you'll just *love* this one Judith! She works in sports!"

"Sports? A woman working in sports? What a waste of time," she says with such aversion that you'd think Elle just told her my job is skinning puppies and kittens alive.

"I'm a sports journalist," I clarify timidly. "I'm actually pretty good at my job."

"You're the tramp from next door dear who has a pathetic crush on my son and somehow managed to divert his eyes momentarily from his wife. But you can say goodbye to any hopes and dreams you had of spending our money because this seedy little affair is over, do you understand?"

"Mum! How fucking *dare* you!" Jacob roars across the room. His dad looks so shocked he nearly falls back into his chair, and his mum looks like she's just been slapped with a wet fish. I'm feeling a rush of things, but mostly I'm gutted that Jacob got there first because I would like to defend myself against her accusations.

I take a step forward and tug Jacob gently by the arm. His breathing is fast and heavy like a wild animal about to pounce. I take a step towards Judith and look her square in the eye.

"I went to university and I worked my butt off and I walked out with a bachelor's degree. I make my own money, and I bought my own house. I have been taking care of myself without poncing off of others for my entire life." I shoot Elle a quick glare to let her know that part was aimed at her. "And above all, I'm smart, smart enough to know that marriages do not work when they aren't about love. I'm smart enough to know that life is too short to worry about status and image. And I'm mature enough to understand that life is about finding the person you want to spend your life with so that you don't end up miserable and bitter and judging everybody else. But above all else, I'm smart enough to know that if I ever have my own children, I will support them in following their own dreams and not mine." And with that, a little voice inside of me says: *Yeah Mia, you really shouldn't have said anything.*

My legs are jelly and my cheeks are burning red, but Jacob is staring at me totally impressed and looking a little like he wants to snog my face off.

If looks could kill, Elle would have me dead right now. Judith looks worried that I managed to find my own voice and stick up for myself – she genuinely looks like nobody has stood up to her before and she doesn't quite know how to react. Jacob's dad is just staring cluelessly like I'm some alien from out of space and he has no idea what I'm going to do next.

And me? I just feel fucking sick.

"Now, if you don't mind," I say calmly as I straighten myself out, "I'm going to be sick in this vase."

And with that, I'm hurling up into a four-foot-tall brown vase in the corner of the dining room that I think is pretty expensive, but right now it is being filled with the orange juice and pasta dish I had on the plane and it really is not a pretty sight.

I feel Jacob's warm hand gently rubbing my back. "Baby, why didn't you say if you were sick?"

I slowly stand up and rub the sick from my chin and try to pull back a smidge of dignity.

"I didn't realise I was."

"Let's get you home." I nod in agreement and try to avoid all eye contact with anyone else as I leave the room.

I can hear Elle tutting behind me. I'm not sure if she's mad that I was sick in her vase or mad that we are leaving which means this scene she had created is over before it had really begun.

"Hang on," I hear Jacob's father call out. I sense some regret in his tone.

"No, Dad. Not now. You have insulted the woman that I love. You belittled her and tried to make fools of us both. It's best you keep your distance for a while." And with that he guides me towards the front door and doesn't look back.

CHAPTER TWENTY-EIGHT

"Where did that come from Rocky?"

"Rocky?"

"Well yeah, I thought you were about to take them all out!" Jacob half laughs as he attempts to make me smile. It works. His smile is infectious.

"Anything else I can do before I go?"

"Hmmm, I think the hot bubble bath you ran, the sandwich you made and unpacking my suitcase was enough."

He pouts at my sarcasm.

He leans over and places a gentle kiss on my moist forehead. I'm still in the bath; I've been in it for twenty minutes and I'm not in a hurry to get out just yet. I feel tired and weak from throwing up earlier. I hope I'm not coming down with something.

Jacob has booked himself into a hotel for the next week or so as a temporary measure until he moves into an apartment in town. Even though he assures me it's best for us all and that he doesn't mind, I can't help but feel guilty knowing he'll be stuck in one small room for a week on his own. After that, I have no clue what is going to happen. We can hardly live together opposite Elle, even if he waited years to move in with me – it's too cruel and unfair.

He promises to message me when he gets to the hotel and we agree to meet tomorrow for dinner.

I listen intently as he gathers his belongings and walks out of the front door. It's strange because I have always very much enjoyed my own space and, after Alex, I expected to be alone for a long time and I was okay with that. My spare time was going to be filled with chatting with Puss and reading smutty novels with a glass of red wine. Oh, Puss. I hadn't thought of her for a little while. I miss her.

When Elle had proudly announced that she had taken Puss away I had wanted to climb across her overpriced dining table and smack her right in between the eyes – but where would that have got me? If she wanted to take it out on me for what has happened, she would have every right to. But to go after a defenceless animal shows her disgusting personality for everything it is.

I actively shut my brain down to stop it from wandering down a negative path. If I allow myself to think this way, I'll only end up anxious before bed. Instead I pull myself from my bubble bath and find a soft airy night dress in my bedroom. I'll make a cup of tea, lock up downstairs and then head to bed. Tonight, I'll fall asleep to Richard Gere and Julia Roberts, although my eyes are so heavy, I doubt I'll even make it to my favourite shopping scene on Rodeo Drive but hey ho.

My phone pings loudly on my nightstand.

I'm at the hotel. Going to shower and get ready for London tomorrow. I'll call you with restaurant reservations in the morning.

P.S NOTICED ANYTHING
NEW IN THE KITCHEN?

I pretty much sprint down the stairs as soon as I see that last sentence. My hair is wet and dripping against my shoulders but I'm not going to hang around and blow dry it when I know a little piece of Jacob is waiting downstairs. What could it be?

I notice it instantly. Hanging up beautifully on my main wall next to the kitchen is our framed photo. It looks even better on the wall than it did when I first saw it. I'm reminded again of how great we look together, how happy and relaxed we are with each other.

It gives me an idea that in time I'd like to have this entire wall filled with photographs. I could probably find more of my mum and get those printed off this week; I'd really like more pictures of her now. I need a new frame for my photo of me and my dad too, I haven't gotten around to replacing it since Alex smashed it. A collage of photos would definitely make me smile every day.

I pop the kettle on and send a little reply to Jacob whilst I wait for it to boil.

> I love it so much. Can't wait to add more
> from our next adventure.

HOPEFULLY A LITTLE LESS DRAMA THIS TIME!

I add a cheeky wink face for good measure and hit send. I grab my favourite mug and reach up for the teabags – why did I store them so high up? I must find a better home for them. Suddenly, everything goes fuzzy and dizzy. The room spins for a moment and I feel funny. Maybe I'm just tired. I must be low on energy. I don't want to stress myself out with any unnecessary worry, so I rationalise that it's probably a mixture of jet lag and tiredness. I grab a custard cream with my tea and head back upstairs.

In the end I don't manage to put on my movie. I slurp my hot tea, eat my biscuit, put the hairdryer through my damp hair until it's dry and get into bed.

***

Bollocks. I check my phone and it's already gone nine a.m. I can't believe I slept through my alarm, I'm so late for work. The only saving grace is that I'm working from home so it's not like I have to jump in the car and fight my way through any traffic, but I should have at least logged onto my computer forty minutes ago. I like to be early and to be prepared. Always have done.
I don't have time to worry about what clothes I'm wearing today, I'll sort myself out on my lunch break. I grab a dressing gown and wrap it around me whilst scuttling down the hallway and into the office. I switch everything on and log in quickly.

I shoot back to my bedroom, grab my empty mug from last night and head downstairs. I'll grab a coffee and a banana and get stuck in. I still don't really have much of an appetite since yesterday's embarrassing vase ordeal.

My photo. I stop in my tracks as I see bits of glass all over the wooden floors. It doesn't take me a second to work out where it has come from. My photo, my beautiful photo that Jacob got me, has shattered. It looks like it has been hit with something small and sharp because there is a perfectly circular puncture hole on my face and surrounding that are bits of cracked glass or missing fragments.

Worryingly, I realise that this isn't accidental and that somebody has done this. I rush to my front door. *Fuck!* I totally forgot to lock it last night. I had that dizzy spell and I was so eager to get to bed that I forgot all about it.
Who would let themselves into my home, take nothing, and destroy just this one item? It must be *Alex.*

I grab my phone from the counter and head straight back out of the front door. What if he is in the house? Has he been there all night? What if he is drunk and going to hurt me? My fingers tremble chaotically as I try to dial Jacob's number. My whole body shivers with nerves. The strong autumnal winds make me colder and shiver even more. Please Jacob, answer.

CHAPTER TWENTY-NINE

Jacob stirs my freshly poured drink and then lightly taps the silver teaspoon against my mug before placing it carefully in the palms of my hands. I'm still shaking, not with anxiety now but more because I'm so cold. I forgot Jacob was in London today – it took him almost two hours to get to me, but I was too afraid to go back indoors so I sat outside the whole time. I contemplated phoning the police but what if they think I'm crazy, panicking so much over one smashed photo? I don't have copies of the notes I was left at the hotel and even if I did, would they take it seriously? There are no direct threats, just abuse. They might even think it's a prank. I don't know, I have never really dealt with the police before.

Jacob checked every cupboard, wardrobe and under my bed when he arrived. He checked the garden, the shed and even the attic. We soon realised that whoever it was must have left pretty quickly after they smashed the photo. There was no sign of a break in, nothing was stolen, nothing else damaged.

"It's not Alex," he gently informs me after I take a sip of my hot tea.
"I found out today, through my contacts, that Alex has been located – he's over five hundred miles away in Brinlack. It's a small village in Northern Ireland. Apparently, he's farming out there, working for some woman."

"Elsbeth," I say, providing the missing piece for him. "She's his aunty. She's a lovely woman. I guess she is getting him the help he needs now."

"I'm sorry Mia, I thought for sure it was him."

"Then it must be Elle," I blurt out, as if the answer was there all along and god knows how we have ignored it all this time.

"I told you Mia, Elle might be eccentric but she's not psychotic. Plus, above all else, she'll be too hammered to pull off such a stunt."

"Then who? Nobody else knows where I live. Nobody else would want to hurt me so much." The panic grows in my voice and Jacob watches on helplessly.

I put my mug down and pace around the lounge. My brain ticks away trying to connect the dots. It *must* be her.

"What about those gang members Elle said you and your dad have been caught up with?"

Jacob's face screws up almost as if to make a mockery of what I have said.

"It's not *funny* Jacob."

"Mia, sweetheart, I promise I'm not mocking you. It's just I think Elle was talking about one of my dad's very old friends who was once part of some North London gang, but it was a long time ago. He's in his seventies now and certainly not a threat. I promise you – I've told you everything about my past, there are no dangerous enemies lurking. That's just Elle stirring the pot."

I anxiously drop my head into my hands. The notes and messages left at the hotel were one thing, but knowing someone has been inside my home whilst I slept is something else entirely.

"Right, let's go talk to Elle," Jacob says. "Come on. Me and you. Let's go."

"And say what? She won't admit it!"

"Maybe not, but it's worth a try. I'll get the truth out of her." Jacob gently tugs me by the hand and leads the way.

I feel very similar to yesterday – sick and ready to run away. I hate this constant back and forth. I almost pray it's not Elle, even though I'm desperate for an answer. I don't want to live opposite someone who is capable of harassing me like this.

Jacob lets himself in with his key and I awkwardly stand in the doorway, not really knowing whether I should follow him in or wait for an invite. I decide to wait. I listen carefully though, expecting to hear Jacob yelling and Elle laughing and revelling in the drama she's caused. Then I imagine Elle firing back with more threats about how Jacob will be disowned by his family and eventually we'll be back to slanging matches.

Oddly though, it's eerily quiet.

"Jacob?" I call but it comes out like a whisper.

Nothing. I don't hear any movement or any voices.

My skin feels like it's covering with goosebumps and my heart pounds harder.

"Jacob?" I call again but this time with more desperation in my voice. I'm freaked out – too much has been happening and I'm on edge. Come on Jacob, just answer me.

I wait another minute or two before deciding to go and investigate. Just as I place one foot inside, Jacob finally appears.

"Sorry, I was reading," he says, startling me when he finally reappears; he holds up a piece of paper and looks pretty baffled.

"What's happened?"

"It's Elle. She's left." His eyebrow arches as if he needed to say it out loud to believe it. "She said that after last night she realised we were beyond repair. She doesn't want the house. She's gone to live with her mum. She's asked me to sell up and give her half of what we make on the house. That's it. She says I'll hear from her solicitor soon."

"Oh?"

"On the plus side, I can sleep in my own bed tonight and leave that hotel."

My brain feels busy with thoughts.

"So, she wasn't here last night?"

Jacob shrugs. "I don't think so."

"Then *who* is it?" I whine before bursting into tears. I must look awful. I noticed earlier that I'm paler than usual; I'm still in my nightdress and my hair hasn't had a brush through it today.

"We'll find out. I'll make some more calls today." Jacob pulls me close to his body and wraps his arms tightly around me. It's re-assuring and comforting but I can't relax into him enough to enjoy it.

"I feel sick again," I mumble. "You may as well head back to work. I'm going to get some more sleep."

"I don't want you to be on your own."

"I'll be fine. You've checked the house. I'll see you tonight?"

"Yes, of course you will. If you're still up for it, I'll take us for dinner. The good news is that I'll be checking out of the hotel later, so I'll be much closer."

I breathe in his cologne as a small smile reaches my cheeks. "That'll make me feel a lot better."

CHAPTER THIRTY

Ten minutes into my nap and someone is knocking on my front door. I'm so tired today and the last thing I want is to have to get out of bed. *Shit.* When I look at my phone, I realise it is well into the afternoon and I haven't been asleep for ten minutes – I have slept for over three hours!

"Coming!" I call out in a wispy voice.

I must look a mess – I have no make-up on, and my hair is scraped up into a high bun. But absolutely not a stylish bun like I hoped – this is more of a Ms Trunchable mop stuck to my head like a bird's nest.

My stomach rumbles loudly as I walk down the stairs. I haven't really eaten all day and as much as I'm hungry, I feel like I could still be sick if I were to even have a bite of something.

Sara? My cousin is holding a huge bouquet of white lilies and her eyes look sad and puffy.

"I'm so sorry to hear about Aunty Tina," she mumbles with the most sorrowful and sympathetic look.

I kind of made my peace with Mum's death while I was in the Bahamas; I didn't even register that family would want to come and pay their respects when I got home.

Sara lunges towards me and pulls me in with a tight hug. "You look like shit," she whispers into my ear.

"Thank you…" I respond with a strong hint of sarcasm.

Sara barges past me and heads straight for the kitchen with the lilies.

"Have you got a vase?"

"Sure, in the bottom cupboard there."

She potters around my kitchen, cutting the stems down and filling the vase with fresh water.

She looks up at me a couple of times and sighs like she is stressed or concerned. Or both.

"What is it?"

"I know your mum just died, but you look really run down. You still have to look after yourself Mia." She looks at me like I'm some helpless child.

"Relax, Sara," I say with some annoyance in my tone. "I made my peace with Mum out in the Bahamas. I got some closure. I was there in her final hours and I said my goodbyes."

She arches her eyebrow at me as if I have just lied to her.

"If that's really the case, then why do you look so awful?"

Her big eyes scan my body up and down as if she is trying to solve some big mystery.

To be honest, her snide digs are starting to grind on me. I don't feel very well, but I don't need to be reminded that I don't look well either.

"I don't know. I've just been sick on and off and feeling dizzy and so, so tired. I honestly think I could sleep for a week."

Sara's face drops.

"Oh god. You're not still messing around with that prick over the road?"

My eyes roll so hard.

"Don't call him that!" I snap. "And why are you looking at me like that?"

"Oh Jesus, Mia. When was your last period?"

"What has that got to do with any... Well, it was..." I pause. I can't actually think that far back. I have been under so much stress lately that I can't even remember when I had a period.

"Has the penny dropped yet?" Sara asks, interrupting my busy mind.

I collapse onto the sofa as I try to work out the possibilities. I have been on birth control for as long as I can remember. I know nothing is ever one hundred percent effective, but surely I'm not pregnant. I can't be. I've been grieving, drinking, I've been stressed. That's hardly a healthy body for a baby. It can't have happened.

"Right then, well whilst you remember how babies are made, I'll pop to the shop and get you a test." And with that she's out of the door and in her car. Suddenly everything is moving at an uncomfortable speed. I have only just realised there could be a possibility and Sara is already one step ahead of me.

I quickly run upstairs and run myself a shower. I need to do something whilst I wait for Sara and this seems like a good place to start. I need to freshen up and sort myself out a little bit. I pour some shampoo into my hands and run it quickly through my hair. A quick body brush and I leap out of the shower. As I bend down to throw a towel around my hair, I get dizzy again and with that comes more nausea. I try to ignore it. I need to get dressed. I throw on a pair of jeans and a cute t-shirt. I already feel a bit better for it. So maybe I'm not pregnant. Maybe I am just run down like I thought.

As I stand by my bedroom window rough drying my hair with my blow-dryer, I see Sara pulling back into my driveaway with a carrier bag beside her on the front seat.

Oh god. I'm going to have to do the test now aren't I? And in front of Sara too, which I dread. No doubt she'll have a judgemental speech to get off her chest before she leaves.

She wastes no time at all as I hear her running up the stairs with her plastic bag ruffling against her hand.

"Ready to wee?"

I shrug.

"I'm not sure, but I guess I can try. Although I can do this later on my own, you don't have to wait with me, I'm sure you have things to do…"

"And miss this?!" she scoffs cruelly. "I don't think so."

I'm getting restless with Sara. I can feel my temper rising again. Since losing Mum, and after all the drama with Alex, I am definitely more impatient than ever. I'm sick of people treating me how they want and thinking they can talk to me how they like. I know how Sara feels about Jacob, she has made it clear before, and I respect her opinion, but it doesn't mean I need to hear it all of the time. Especially right now. She hands me the test and stares at me as if this is the best gossip she's had all year.

"I hope for your sake it's negative."

"Excuse me?"

"Well come on, it sounds like you were only a bit of skirt to distract him from his failing marriage. Do you really think a baby is what he signed up for?" She laughs loudly at her own rhetorical question as if she is ever so witty and clever.

And it really pisses me off.

I snatch the test out of her hand and lock myself in the bathroom. I perch on the edge of the toilet seat and just take a moment for myself.

CHAPTER THIRTY-ONE

"I haven't taken the test yet," I answer as Sara knocks on the door for the fourth time.

I'm lying of course. The test is sitting beside me on the bathroom floor. I just haven't plucked up the courage to look.

I'm not sure what I am most afraid of. The results or Sara's attitude.

"I'm coming in…"

"No wait! I can't pee if you're in here gawping at me; just five more minutes please."

"Ugh, fine," she huffs outside the bathroom door.

I don't think Sara is going to give me much more time before she tries barging in here to see what the hold-up is. I definitely don't want to read the results with her beside me. I reach out and take hold of the test, leaving it face down.

I cradle it delicately on my lap. Whatever the results are, I can handle it. I have been through the most challenging year of my life and I am still here. I can cope with whatever this says.

My heart is skipping beats; I take a breath in and slowly exhale.

I flip the test over and stare down at the little white stick.

Two little pink lines are clearly showing in the tiny window. Two little lines have just changed my life.

I'm pregnant.

"Can I come in yet?" I hear Sara faintly call in the background, but I can barely grasp it. I'm too shocked.

"Mia?!?" Her voice is raised and bossy like she is going to lose her temper with me.

I slide across the bathroom floor, reach up and unlock it before sitting back down. The door flies open almost instantly.

"About time – I have never known anyone take so long to pee!"

I don't even look up at her, my eyes stay fixed on the two pink lines.

"Oh fuck, you are, aren't you?" Her voice is high pitched like she's had the shock of the century. "Fuck, Mia! He's gotten you pregnant, hasn't he?"

"*Gotten* me pregnant? Jeez. You make it sound seedy. It was both of us Sara. It takes two to tango as they say."

"However you want to word it, he won't stick around Mia. I know his type. Good luck being a single mum – you'll need it."

"You don't know *anything* Sara. He's a good man and he loves me."

"Pah! How do you know that? I bet he says that to anyone who pays him attention."

"He flew to the Bahamas to be with me didn't he?"

"Didn't you say he had booked the Bahamas for a holiday anyway? So, he already wanted to get you away on his own. He probably saw Aunty Tina dying as a great result – it was an excuse to have a sordid getaway with you."

I stand up instantly – I have to get away from her before I do something I regret. How dare she?

"He stood by my side every step of the way and at times it wasn't pretty! I really struggled out there and he kept me sane. So please, save your judgemental comments. You know nothing."

I head straight down the stairs and into the kitchen. I need a cold bottle of water and I need Sara to go home. I can't handle any more stress from her.

Annoyingly, the second I close the refrigerator door, I find Sara has followed me down and is standing with her hands on her hips.

"Mia, I'm sorry. I'm just trying to make you see."

"But you don't know him!"

"He is a typical cheat. He hurt his wife and guess what? He'll hurt you too!"

I can't even answer her. I down the water as quickly as I'm physically able to. I don't ever remember feeling so thirsty before. This must be a pregnancy symptom.

When I swallow the last gulp and get my breath back, Sara is still standing in the same way, looking like she is ready for some kind of back-and-forth argument. I knew she had an arrogant streak but acting like she knows every little thing in mine and Jacob's relationship really tops it.

"Okay..." I begin calmly. "I appreciate your warning, but this is my life and I'll do what I think is best. Right now, Jacob is going through a divorce and so he doesn't need the extra stress. I will tell him in a couple of months that I am having his baby and, if he chooses to leave, I will accept that, and I will love this baby because no matter what, it is mine."

"Pfft. Why are you giving him time? He got himself into his situation. He should know."

"And he will! When I am ready and when I know he is ready." I steady myself against the refrigerator as another dizzy spell takes hold of me.

Sara seems to notice my struggle and finally offers some care.

"When did you last eat?"

"This morning, I had a banana."

"That won't be enough. Not if you're eating for two. Sit down on the sofa, I'll make you a sandwich."

This is the side of Sara I like. When she chooses to be my supportive caring cousin, I adore her, like I always have. Then again, I have never done anything like this before for her to judge me on. I hope she changes her attitude soon because I love nothing more than having her around when she is like this. I watch her make me a sandwich with salad bits, fresh ham and a slice of thick cheese – just how I like it. She cuts up some apples and places them on the side of my plate and cleans up after herself as she goes.

"Cup of tea too?"

I nod. "Yes please."

"I'll pop a sugar in to keep your strength up."

"Thank you." I smile gratefully. For the first time in this whole hour we seem to be getting along like normal.

She passes me the plate and I nibble suspiciously at the crust; I have no idea whether this sandwich will make me feel better or make me sick again.

Another grumble and hunger pangs take over my tummy which pushes me to take a big bite. I must admit, it tastes delicious and within minutes I have demolished it.

"You must have needed that!" Sara smiles as she places a cup of tea in front of me.

"I'm tired again…" I sigh.

"You will be – the first trimester sucks. Enjoy your sore boobs, sickness and tiredness won't you," she smirks playfully.

I giggle but then a thought takes over that stops me instantly. "I do wish my mum was here though. And my dad. They'd be awesome grandparents."

"They'll be looking down and watching proudly, I bet."

It makes me wonder a little more in depth. Will this baby have any grandparents around as it's growing up? It's not like Jacob's mum or dad were thrilled about us, I can't imagine a baby will impress them. Would they even want to be in the baby's life? Or would they choose to boycott us completely? I worry how that might make Jacob feel. I need to stop overthinking. What will be will be.

"Loverboy is back," Sara announces as she peers out of the window like a nosey neighbour. "Oh, and he's heading straight this way."

I awkwardly play with my hair and try to compose myself. Hopefully no more dizzy spells take over me.

I'm hoping Sara will grab her bag and leave as she and Jacob definitely do not get along, but instead, she heads back into the kitchen and boils the kettle again. This doesn't bode well for me.

"Hey beautiful!" Jacob adoringly smiles before placing a kiss on my head.
"I missed you today."

"Coffee Jakey?" Sara calls before I even have a second to respond.

His face immediately drops, and his eyes darken as if he is a wild animal in the woods that just bumped into a hunter with a gun.

"No thanks, I've had about all the caffeine I can cope with today."

"Fair enough. How was your holiday?" She says it in a way that indicates she is testing Jacob already. She'll wait for him to answer and then her brain will be busy analysing everything he says.

"Well, it was hardly a holiday, but the island was beautiful if that's what you're asking."

"Hmm-mm," she replies, clearly unsatisfied with his response. "How's the wife?"

"Ex-wife?"

"Sure." She smiles but her smugness and arrogance are all too obvious. She is trying to goad Jacob and we both know it.

"What would that have to do with you Sara? I am sure Mia has told you we have started our divorce proceedings; we're separated, so I don't really know how she is. Nor is it my problem." His jaw is clenched, and his demeanour is defensive. The two of them are ready for war.

"Okay, no need to get testy. I just like to take an interest since we are all going to be family soon."

Jacob looks confused and I can tell he doesn't know how to respond. He stares at Sara as if he doesn't have a clue what she is talking about.

"What?" he snaps impatiently. "I really don't have time for your games today."

I shake my head desperately in the background, but Sara chooses to ignore it.

"It's not a game Jakey. Everybody knows that there's nothing like a baby to bring us all together."

Fuck Sara! How could she? *Why* would she? I told her my plans and she has just showed me that she doesn't care at all about them. She'd rather get one over on Jacob than respect my fucking wishes.

Jacob looks back at me, his jaw dropping open. His eyes narrow into mine as if he is trying to find the answers in them.

"Sorry," I sob. "I only just found out myself! I'm so sorry," I repeat desperately.

"It's okay Jakey, I've got this. So you can run along now and find a new bit of skirt to play with."

"You're pregnant?" He looks so shocked and off guard; I hate the way Sara has thrown this at him. Hate it. I nod sadly. This is the worst way he could have found out.

"Bye bye Jakey. Have a nice life."

"Sara, when will you get it through your thick skull that I'm in love with Mia and I'm not going anywhere? You know, at first I thought you really were the concerned cousin, but now I can see that you're clearly just jealous."

He gets to his feet and steps towards her. His anger is growing and his voice deepens to a growl.

Sara backs away timidly, but it looks like Jacob has just hit a nerve.

"Yeah. That's it isn't it? You're jealous. Perhaps you are also in a loveless marriage."

"Don't be so ridiculous! We are childhood sweethearts," she proudly fires back.

"Maybe it's the baby thing then. Maybe you've been trying and trying with no luck and suddenly Mia is pregnant out of the blue and you can't handle it?"

"Fuck off!" Sara scowls.

Oh god. That's it. Jacob found her nerve.

"Both of you, please stop!"

"Why? These are his true colours Mia! Why stop now?"

"My true colours? You do nothing but belittle people you claim to love – you're so fucking bored in your shitty little life that you judge others to make you feel better!"

"That's it! Mia. Choose. Ultimatum time – your family, or this disgrace of a human."

"For god's sake, it doesn't have to be like this!" I stand in between them, trying to create some distance.

"Yes, it does! Choose! Tell him to get out once and for all!"

"Please Sara, stop!" Another dizzy spell takes over me and all I want to do is sit back down.

Jacob is staring at Sara in disbelief – if she was a man, he might have punched her by now. His tongue rubs against his bottom lip before he bites down. I can tell he is trying to restrain himself from laying into her even more.

"Come on, Mia! Find your voice for god's sake. Tell him to get out."

"Fine! GET OUT," I shout so loudly that even I surprise myself.

"What?" Jacob's voice drops sorrowfully as he gently tugs at my arm as if to plead with me. I can see Sara's smug smirk in the corner of my eye as she folds her arms and tilts her head as if she is waiting patiently for Jacob to leave.

"Not you," I breathe. "Get out Sara."

Now it's her jaw dropping. She looks bewildered.

"Now. I'm done Sara – get the fuck out of my house," I scream again which shocks her.

Jacob holds onto me tightly; he must have sensed my dizziness. I lean into him and get my breath back.

The tension is thick and uncomfortable. I turn my head into Jacob's shoulder; I can't even look at Sara anymore.

"Goodbye, Mia," I hear before a slamming of the door.

CHAPTER THIRTY-TWO

It's Friday. Thankfully the dizziness has passed and although I am still nauseous, I feel so much better.

Jacob has been a real support since Sara selfishly announced my pregnancy to him like some planned ambush. The timing couldn't have been worse – Jacob had a client who had absconded from court and when they finally caught up with him, he was at a train station in Liverpool. Jacob had no choice but to travel up to him and attempt to ease the situation before it got any worse. Therefore, we have had barely any time to talk and I have just had to assume that he is fine with the idea of a baby. He has been wonderful and supportive towards me though, as best he can. I have had several text messages reminding me to drink lots of water and take it easy, but I just wish I could know what he is thinking. Is he ready to be a father? Is he excited? Is he scared?

These are things that I won't know until he comes home tomorrow night. The wait is an anxious one, but I am doing my best to keep my intrusive thoughts at bay.

I spend my morning working from my office and as soon as lunchtime comes around, I click onto Google and begin online shopping. At first it is just necessities: I search for a new photo frame to replace the one that got smashed, then I look for a new hairdryer – mine is getting so old that I'm convinced it is going to blow up any day now.

Then, curiosity gets the better of me, and I start to search for nursery items. So many adorable things pop up: little crib mobiles with hanging zoo animals and night lights that project stars onto the ceiling, the tiniest little sleepsuits with sheep on them and fancy Moses baskets with drapes on either side. It gives me a tingly sensation in my tummy – a kind of excitement and anxiety all in one, but mostly an eagerness; it's like I want to buy it all and give my baby the best I possibly can.

I wonder which Moses basket Jacob would prefer and whether he'd choose the sleepsuits with sheep on them or the ones with stars. I can't imagine him brooding over a baby. He has a hard exterior and although I have seen his softer side, I don't know how easily it will come to him to extend that to a baby.

A loud thunder-style banging sounds against my front door just as I'm getting stuck into my next work task. It startles me and instantly I feel worry and dread over who it could be. It definitely wasn't a friendly knock – if there ever was the perfect way to intimidate someone just by knocking that would certainly be it.

I lean out of the window and peer down to my front door, but I can't see anyone standing there. *Please* don't be Sara. Surely even she wouldn't come back this quickly – either with her tail between her legs, or worse, looking for another argument. A heavy sigh falls from my lips as I make my way down the stairs. *Please* don't be Sara.

I reluctantly pull open my front door; a gust of autumn wind blows a bunch of brown crunchy leaves over my feet, but nobody is there. I wait a moment as if expecting someone to reappear – and that is when I notice it. Out of the corner of my eye, I see an envelope pinned to my front door by a rusty nail. I realise that the thunder-like pounding was actually a hammer, beating this nail into my door. Immediately, this fills me with an uneasiness. Something really doesn't feel right about this. I pull at the nail and wriggle it several times before it eventually slides out of the wood and releases the envelope.

Instantly, I slam the door shut and slide the bolt across the top. My heart pounds as I do. I remember when I was a child, if ever I went downstairs in the night to get a drink, I would always run back up the stairs as fast as I could so that the monsters couldn't get me. I have a very similar feeling now. My hands tremble in fear that there might be a monster behind my door and the only thing separating us is this bolt.

I glance out through each of the windows – the wind is wild today, leaves are being thrown against the glass and branches are swinging dramatically, but I can't see anybody lurking. I do, however, feel like I am being watched, enough that it prompts me to close all the drapes along the large full-length windows and pray that it is enough to give me privacy.

The only thing I am sure about is that whoever is out there has left me this envelope. I stare down at it, searching for answers before I open it. It's blank. There is no writing on it, it is not addressed to anyone.

I pace across the kitchen. Carefully, I pull open the tab and brace myself as I do. Inside is a photo. Nothing else, just one small polaroid-style photograph.

My hands shake dramatically as I slide it out to reveal what it could be.

Rubble. Mud. Grass. Fur. Blood. So much blood. *Puss.*

"PUSS!" I choke as I throw the photo away from me. My breathing is fast and hard, my chest has gone tight and I'm fighting for breath. My eyes swell instantly, and tears pour effortlessly down my face.

"Oh, god! Poor Puss," I wail. "No, no, no. Not sweet Puss!"

I can barely fathom what I have just looked at. The way sweet innocent Puss was lying. I feel horrible acidic stomach bile rising to my throat. I lean across to the sink just in time as I violently vomit, my throat being scratched in the process. The bile burns and stings against my throat which makes me sweat and struggle for breath. I sound wheezy. My throat is so thick and sore it's restricting my breathing.

It's a panic attack Mia. Count to ten. Visualise something else, anything else. Visualise the beautiful spring day when you moved in. Remember that happy time.

It seems to take the edge off for a split second but then I remember how I met Puss that day and how she kept me company. I remember how lonely I had felt but how having Puss around helped with that.

And with that thought, I'm back to square one. I squeeze my eyes tightly shut, hoping to push away the image of Puss.

Poor Puss. She looked like she was hit with a car, or a *hammer*.

Stop Mia, you're scaring yourself. Deep breaths.

Whoever did this is the same person who sent me those notes. I know it. Whoever it is knows how to hurt me. They know about Puss. They knew I loved her.

CHAPTER THIRTY-THREE

"Well you're absolutely not staying here on your own anymore," Jacob declares, making it clear that I don't have a choice.

I don't argue. I barely slept a wink last night and every time I felt my eyes close and my body relax, I heard those same bangs hammering against my front door. Of course, it was my mind playing tricks on me, but at four o'clock in the morning it certainly feels real.

"This is sick. This isn't just a stalker; this is someone deranged or dangerous. Probably both."

"I know." My voice strains, still sore from yesterday.

"Whoever it is has a fucking death wish. They're not just hurting you; they're hurting my baby. This stress won't be good for him."

"Him?" I smile despite myself.

"Just a guess!" he shrugs and smiles back.

This is the first time he has spoken of the baby since he found out about it, and it instantly pulls at my heart strings and fills me with a warmth I haven't experienced before. The way he already cares so much for our unborn baby tells me everything I need to know about the type of father I can expect him to be. Unlike his own dad, he is going to love our child unconditionally.

Jacob stares down at the photo again in disgust. He paces the living room and all I hear are more swear words and threats being muttered under his breath.

"We should move away," he finally says. "I can't be here to protect you all the time and we can't live like this. My baby can't grow up in a place where some psycho murders cats and pins the fucking evidence on the front door."

"But I *love* this house. This place is the first big thing I achieved on my own and it's home."

"Then at the very least, you need to leave here for a couple of months until I find the arsehole responsible. Maybe see if you can stay at a friend's house or something."

I can see his thoughts busying his mind. He paces back and forth, running his hand through his hair and then gripping it in frustration.

"What about our baby? I don't want to go through this pregnancy without you close by."

"Neither do I, but for fuck's sake Mia, meet me halfway! I can't risk either of you being harmed."

"I'm not going anywhere, Jacob." I say it with such authority that he knows I won't budge on this decision.

"Do you have to be a stubborn pain in the ass today?"

I soften my approach in the hope that I can calm him down. I take a step towards him and place my hands gently on either side of his chiselled torso.

"Jacob, I can't let this person win. I'm scared, yes. But I won't let them run me out of my own home. This is where I belong."

He sighs at my perseverance but quickly drops his arms from behind his head and wraps them around my waist instead. He pulls me in close, breathing in the scent of my hair in the process.

"Fine. But you stay with me, in my house, at least for a few weeks whilst I pile on the pressure to this private investigator and find this fucking arsehole."

I nod into his arms. We have reached a compromise and although I know he isn't happy about it, he is allowing me this small victory and I love him for it. I love so much that he wants us to be safe.

Jacob helps me pack a suitcase, even though I protest that I can just pop back if I need anything. He feels strongly that he doesn't want me doing that on my own and so it is better if I just take everything I need now. I don't push back on it.

By dinner time, I'm freshly showered, in a comfortable lounge suit and Jacob is dishing up some tomato tagliatelle with chicken and chorizo.

"What, no wine tonight?" I tease as he serves me a huge portion.

He forces a frown, but I keep smiling until eventually he can't hold it any longer and his gorgeous smile makes an appearance.

"No. But you can have a glass of milk."

"Milk? With my pasta?"

"Yes, I read that you need to keep your calcium levels up, as well as your B12 – and are you taking folic acid?"

I giggle at his serious tone.

"Folic acid?"

"Yes, it's a vitamin that you're supposed to take in the first trimester."

"I know what folic acid is! But how do you!?"

"I did some reading on the train to Liverpool," he answers, suddenly blushing as if he already knows I'm about to coo over this.

And of course, I do.

"Aww! Jacob!"

"Shut up, you!" He playfully nudges me. "I just want my baby to have the best start."

My heart melts at his words and at the thought of him research-
ing pregnancy and babies on the train. I'm not sure what I expected from Jacob, but I know this exceeds it.

After dinner, Jacob suggests an early night and it's easily the best
decision of the day. I am exhausted. I think all in all I managed
about an hour of sleep last night and I have definitely paid for it
today. My face looks pale and I feel as though I could be hungover.

I head upstairs; Jacob is already stripped down to his black boxers and brushing his teeth in the en-suite.

I stare at his bed, the bed he shared with Elle for so many years.
The thought of him lying next to her, cuddling her, possibly even
being intimate with her is too much for my jealousy. I can't handle the thought.

"I don't think I can sleep in this bed… it wouldn't be right."

Jacob pauses what he is doing and looks at the bed momentarily
before he works out what I am probably thinking.

"I understand…"

He finishes up and leads me out of the bedroom by the hand. We
walk down the hall, past his office and into a beautifully decor-
ated black and white bedroom. The walls are white, apart from
one which is matte black. The bed frame is matte black, the bedding is black, and the majority of the ornaments are black. On
paper it might sound a bit too dark and gloomy but it's actually
very stylish. Typical Elle. The girl definitely knows how to style
a room.

"I know what you're thinking but this is actually my room. I
styled it. Well, with the help of one of Elle's designers, but I did it.
It's mine."

I feel so much better knowing that this was an Elle-free zone.

Jacob pulls back the black duvet and gestures me to get in. I oblige. He quickly climbs over me and buries himself under the duvet beside me. His warm skin against mine is heavenly and relaxes me instantly.

"Do you feel safe?" he whispers into the nape of my neck.

I nod. I do – so safe in fact that I can already feel my heavy eyes closing and my body relaxing against his.

"Good. Close your eyes beautiful. Get some rest." His hand reaches around the front of my tummy and his thumb gently strokes just below my belly button, almost as if he is comforting our baby too. I wish I could bottle this moment and save it forever. It is perfect.

CHAPTER THIRTY-FOUR

I'm awoken the next morning by the glorious smell of breakfast cooking. The last two days I have been constantly hungry so my mouth instantly waters at the thought of thick white buttery toast and eggs with a runny yolk. I throw on a chunky knit jumper and head downstairs. It's another cold crisp autumn day outside by the looks of it. Plenty of orange and brown leaves are swirling around the garden.

"Have you got any plans for today?" Jacob asks cheerfully as he scoops an egg up with his spatula and carefully places it on some toast.

Okay, I am seriously impressed with my sense of smell right now. I knew exactly what it was going to be from upstairs. I sit up at the kitchen island on the high stool and look at my plate hungrily.

"I'm free as a bird," I answer as I start getting stuck into my breakfast.

"Good, because I have a surprise for you."

"Oooh, I'm intrigued! Do I get any clues as to where we are going?"

"Newsflash Mia, usually the idea of a surprise is that you're not supposed to have a clue!"

I playfully screw my face up at his unwillingness to share any details. I'm rubbish at surprises myself, I can never keep my cool and I always end up dropping far too many clues and giving things away.

Jacob places a hot mug of tea next to my plate – just when I thought my breakfast couldn't get any better.

I smile at him adoringly; I hope he knows how much I appreciate this.

Jacob fills his own plate and takes a seat next to me, and together we enjoy our breakfast and barely speak. The only sound is the wind whistling past the window. It's oddly comforting. It's the kind of weather that makes you want to get snuggly under a knitted blanket and sip hot chocolates.

Jacob remains tight-lipped in the car – the only clue I have is that we are driving further into the countryside. Usually, we head towards town and I can't think of what could be in this direction. The windscreen wipers slide backwards and forwards as the cool crisp morning has turned into a rainy wet midday.

I look around in anticipation, hoping for at least one clue. Jacob catches me a few times and laughs. He loves it when he holds all the cards, mostly because he knows how impatient I am.

"If it helps, we are only three miles away."

"And then where will we be? On the set of the film *Deliverance*?" I joke just to see his smile and it works.

I slide my hand over and rest it on his thigh. If today is an example of what is to come in our new life together then I can't wait to wake up every morning. I'm already imagining decorating Christmas trees with him and making alcoholic snowball cocktails whilst we sing along to Mariah Carey and Wham and hang our stockings over the fireplace. I imagine taking our baby on their first holiday, imagining Jacob's and the baby's little toes in the thick cream sand, building sandcastles and giggling when we knock them down again. I imagine taking hundreds of new photos, capturing memories and coming home to hang them on my wall to remind myself every day of how lucky I am. The excitement swirls up inside me. My future looks the best it has ever looked.

"Here we are..." Jacob announces as we drive into a gravelly car park with a sign that reads *Last Chance.*

What on earth is Last Chance?

I notice ahead of us that there are multiple pet shelters and before I make the connection, Jacob confirms it for me.

"We are going to rehome a cat. Give one of these little guys a loving home; and I know how lucky they'll be to have you. I'm not saying it'll replace Puss, but I think our first pet and a little extra company will be just what you need."

I lean across and plant a kiss on his cheek; he is being so thoughtful. This gesture is so sweet and kind it makes me want to cry. That could be partly pregnancy hormones, but I am so touched all the same.
I feel like a kid in a sweet shop as I stride excitedly towards the shelter. My face lights up at the realisation I get to take one of these beautiful cats home today.

We joke and banter as we read some of the descriptions.

"Ah, this one doesn't like men..." I read with a big smirk across my face. The idea of rehoming a man-hating cat could be quite handy for a lot of women!

"Oh ha-ha." Jacob's sarcasm is rife. "Maybe we can find one that doesn't like ex-wives..."

"...and new mothers-in-law!"

"Touché!" Jacob smirks and we both laugh in unison. "We could get a ginger one and name it Ron Weasley!"

"Or we could get a white one and call it Snowball!" I add, matching Jacob's ridiculous suggestion.

Soon, we approach a gorgeous petite black cat with a white spot on its nose. Jacob and I both look at each other straight away –

she's unique and quirky. We already love her.

I nod at Jacob and he looks pretty impressed with himself that he chose the right place today.

"She's the one then!" he agrees before disappearing to find one of the shelter employees to help us.

I stay staring at her – she's beautiful. She comes right up to the metal fence and rubs her head against it as if she wants my attention and to say hello. I poke my fingers through and scratch around her ears and she purrs heavily.

"Well pretty little girl, I think I'll name you Autumn. Because that is when we found you and, just like autumn, you are beautiful."

A disturbing image of Puss flashes into my brain and makes me shudder. I won't let Autumn out of my sight – if need be, she'll be an indoor cat for a while. I can't let her explore the neighbourhood until Jacob finds out who the hell it is who is stalking me. Or finally admits it is Elle. Because I'm tired of pretending I don't believe it is her. She was the last person to see Puss after all. She practically told us by posting that photo of Puss that it is her. But I don't think Jacob is ready to accept the truth.

CHAPTER THIRTY-FIVE

Autumn settles in well considering she has had to spend half an hour in the car and is now in a brand-new home with lots of new smells and things to see. I offer to cook but Jacob suggests a take-away and this option does sound more appealing. After some back and forth discussions we settle on an Indian takeaway. I order my favourite Rogan Josh and Jacob opts for a spicy Madras.

It feels strange spending another night here – it feels so wrong, like I am overstepping the line. This was Elle's house as well. But then I think about how Jacob paid for this entire house and everything in it so I guess if he wants me here then it should be okay. I can hardly go back to my house right now anyway.

I take my plate of delicious-smelling curry and get comfortable in the armchair; I curl up with my legs tucked up and pull a blanket over my lap.

"What?" Jacob is staring at me.

"Nothing. It's just really nice to see you so relaxed." He grabs his plate and sits opposite me on the sofa. "I can't remember the last time I ate dinner on the sofa."

"Oh shit! Sorry, we can go to the table, I just didn't think."

Jacob gestures frantically for me to sit back down. "No, no! I didn't mean that. I just meant that Elle would be very strict about eating at the table; she would never allow us to be this casual… It's just, I don't know, it's just real. I love that about you."

I pretend not to find him quite as adorable as I do, and I dig into my curry.

We spend the next hour and a half watching *Die Hard*, although most of the film is spent arguing about whether it is a Christmas film or not. I'm adamant it isn't, but Jacob strongly believes I am wrong.

By the end of the movie I can't stop yawning. Jacob notices and orders me to bed.

He peels back the duvet cover for me and ushers me in as if I am some delicate and fragile little thing. I give him a sideways glance and smile.

"It's okay, I'm pregnant, I'm not dying." I love mocking him, I'm sure I'm the only one who gets away with it. His arrogance and hard outer shell mean that he would tear into most people who dare banter with him in this way, but with me, I think he secretly gets a kick out of it.

"I know, but if I don't keep an eye on you, you tend to do odd things like vomit into people's vases."

"Seriously? That was one time."

"And yet it was so momentous. And in front of my parents too who were meeting you for the first time..." His eyes narrow, waiting for me to react.

It works, I'm burying my head under the duvet and squealing with embarrassment. "Fuck off!"

"Now, now, Miss Johnson, watch your mouth otherwise I'll have to add Tourette's to your glowing cv. No wonder my parents looked gobsmacked."

"Piss off!" I screech again and playfully kick against his legs under the duvet. I hear him laughing, pleased with himself that he has gotten under my skin. His hands reach out to find me and he carefully places one hand across my ribcage.

When I whip the duvet away from my face, I notice him staring away into space, looking lost in thought and sad.

"What's wrong?" I sit up quickly and lean closer to him, but he doesn't break his gaze, he just shrugs instead.

"Come on, you do know. What's going on?"

He shuffles restlessly beside me. "It's just, I don't know, I'm scared." He turns over to face me, his face so close to mine that I can feel his breath against my skin. "I worry that people will always say that we are nothing more than a silly affair."

"Who says that?"

"Well, Sara for one. My fucking parents for another. It's like, I couldn't really give a shit what anyone else has to say about us. They don't know how I feel. They have no idea that I felt as though I could fall in love with you from the moment I heard you swearing at your bloody vacuum cleaner, the way you answered the door, dripping wet in your white towel, hilariously awkward but so charismatic with it. They don't know that I spent the next several days thinking non-stop about how beautiful your eyes were, or how I'd rip apart anyone who would ever try to hurt you, like Patrick and *fucking* Alex. They don't know that this is the most I have ever felt for anyone else in my entire life.

"Our child will be in this world soon, and I'd hate for him to grow up hearing dickheads refer to us as some naughty affair that should have never lasted. It will hurt me deeply for my son to ever believe for just a second that I don't love and adore his mum with every fibre of my being. And yes, maybe how we started wasn't conventional and orthodox, but I couldn't keep away. There was no way we were ever going to be just neighbours. I knew you were different; I knew I wanted to have you. Not just once but for good. And I damn well knew I didn't want anyone else to have you."

His words are soft and genuine and make me smile from ear to ear. His protectiveness gives me butterflies in my stomach and makes my heart skip.

"Our son, *or daughter,* will always know how much we love each other. They will know that they were born out of nothing but love."

Jacob drops his head so that his forehead is gently resting against mine.

"God, I love you so much Mia."

His mouth slightly opens, and he kisses me delicately, sliding his tongue against mine at the very first opportunity. His plump lips never fail to excite me. I softly groan into his mouth, indulging this very moment.

"Can we… you know?" He points to my tummy, unsure.

"Of course we can…" I resist making a sarcastic comment.

"And it won't hurt you or the baby or anything?" My head shakes and I pull him closer to me, pressing his strong toned frame against me.

His hands quickly entwine with mine and he raises them above my head and presses them into the pillow; he uses that leverage to pull himself on top of me. I turn my head to gently kiss his biceps whilst he whispers into the side of my neck how much he loves me.

He frees one hand and drags his fingers up from the side of my calf to my hip, his fingertips electrifying my skin. He pulls my leg up and hugs my thigh as he slowly enters me; my thigh clings against his waist. I enjoy watching his muscular arms hold on to me so tightly. I feel weightless in his grip and Jacob knows I love it too. He smiles as he watches me groan and bite down onto my bottom lip. He gets a kick out of knowing what he can do to me. He knows he is the only one who has ever been able to make me melt like this. I wind my hips against his and take my free hand into his hair, tugging at it roughly. I know he enjoys it because he rolls his head back, looking up at the ceiling momentarily to delay himself from finishing. Now I'm smiling, knowing full well I can end him anytime I want.

CHAPTER THIRTY-SIX

I wake up dead on three a.m. I only know this because Jacob's ridiculously bright alarm clock beams next to me. I have woken up so thirsty again, but this time I crave icy cold water. I can almost imagine myself eating a bag of ice cubes straight out of the freezer. I had no idea cravings could come on so quickly. I very slowly climb out of bed, careful not to wake Jacob who is peacefully resting beside me, sprawled out with his messy dark hair flopped over to one side. He looks like a bloody model even at this time of night. I, on the other hand, look like an escaped lunatic with cholera. Thank god for Charlotte Tilbury and her fantastic make-up line, or I think I'd have been single forever.

I see Autumn curled up in a tight ball at the bottom of the stairs. We did buy her a bed, well two actually, but I guess she prefers that little space on the floor. Her eyes flicker as I creep down the stairs, and she stretches her paws out with a yawn, but she doesn't move much or seem phased by me having to step over her.

Result – my prayers have been answered. In the side door of the refrigerator is one of those water jug filter things. Personally, I've never understood the hype with them – surely water straight out of the tap is just as good but I won't complain – it's fresh and, more importantly, it's cold. I almost jump for joy with how cold it feels when I take it from the fridge. Unfortunately, I can't seem to find the ice cubes I hoped for, but this will do.

The icy water quickly refreshes my dry sticky throat and I let out a sigh of relief after I knock back an entire glass of the gorgeously chilled water. Much better.

I hover, deciding if I need another glassful, but I don't want to be up all night peeing. Autumn appears in the kitchen doorway and glides so delicately towards me. She's so petite and classy; her black fur shines under the dim light from the swimming pool and her purrs are heavy as she rubs herself against my shin.

Wow, I have a boyfriend, a baby on the way and a cat. How did this happen so quickly? If I have learned anything from my mum, it is that life can be so short, so just enjoy it. I'm grateful and I'm lucky. I have everything I ever wanted but never thought I could get. Alex called me broken goods enough times that it soon became what I believed I was – but here I am. I'm not broken, I'm not damaged, I'm not baggage. I'm happy.

When I stand up, I realise that the swimming pool lights look different somehow. I can't seem to focus on them like I could just ten minutes ago. They're brighter, but blurrier and I'm finding it hard to focus on them. My eyes feel weak. I can't really describe it, but I know I feel odd; I don't feel right at all. Could it be another unfortunate side effect of pregnancy? I'm not sure, but now my head feels heavy and it's an effort to hold myself up. My brain feels foggy and tired. My hands feel as though they're going numb and then, terrifyingly, I realise I can't feel my lips.

Autumn meows at me as I stumble into the kitchen island and try my best to steady myself, but I feel as though I'm on a boat in some rough seas. I can't seem to hold my balance. Her meows are becoming muffled as if I'm underwater and my vision is getting blurrier, not just with lights, but with everything around me.

Fuck, what is happening?

I manage to step to the patio doors, my legs wobbling beneath me, threatening to give way at any time.

I frantically fight with the lock until I release it and the patio door swings open. I step barefoot onto the grass, hoping the cold fresh air will snap me out of this, but I can barely feel the air. I should – it's autumn now, it's much colder at night. I realise

I'm starting to sweat profusely and pure panic jolts through my body as I succumb to the fact that something awful is happening to me.

I scream for Jacob, but I have no idea if I'm even making a sound. It's too hard to scream and shout. It's like I physically cannot put my body through that much effort, but I can't give up trying. The garden around me spins and sways and I'm grabbing around for something to hold onto before I fall and hurt myself. I see the silver handrail by the swimming pool steps, and I pray that if I can just hold onto it, I can steady myself and keep calling for Jacob.

Another small step closer but I can't see the handrail anymore, I can't focus enough to find it. It was here, I'm sure it was, what happened? My hands are stretched out in front of me, trying to feel for the safety of that rail, but nothing.

Suddenly, my surroundings are darker, quieter. Water fills my ears and deafens me. Holy fuck. I think I'm in the swimming pool. I've fallen. I kick my legs frantically to jolt myself back to the surface, but my efforts are futile. I flap my arms, but it does nothing but weigh me down. My tired body feels like it is filled with bricks and I'm just sinking further down and down into the water. My brain confuses me. I'm not sure what's happening anymore. My eyes are closing. My body stops jolting. I stop trying. Everything goes black.

***

"She's pregnant too!"

"I know sir, you already told us that."

"She'll be okay right? And the baby too?"

"It's too soon to tell…"

"Why hasn't she woken up yet!?"

"Sir, I need you to take a step back."

"Mia! Mia, baby, wake up. I'm here, okay, I'm right here and I'm not going anywhere!"

"Sir…"

"Stay with me, Mia!"

"Sir, I need you to take a step back and let us do our job."

"Just save her! Just please fucking save her!"

CHAPTER THIRTY-SEVEN

"What do you mean they came from my address? I was in the Bahamas with her… Wait, what? Fucking what!?"

I feel like I have just woken up from the deepest sleep of my life, but I can't yet open my eyes or move my body. I still feel so heavy and zapped of energy, but it's like my brain is switched on again. I can hear things. I can hear machines beeping around me and muffled conversations somewhere in the distance, but mostly I can hear Jacob: he is angry, beyond angry, and it makes me uneasy. I don't understand what is happening.

"How the hell could she be some sick bitch and I not know about it? This is all my fault."

The beeps around me get a little faster as I listen to Jacob's voice, listening for answers about what is going on, what has happened to me.

"I don't need to fucking sit down, just tell me what you know. Tobias, tell me!"

He must be too loud because I hear a faint shushing from the other side of the room. I can't see her, but I assume it's a nurse.

"Where? Where was her phone tracked? Tonight? But it can't have been. I thought she left for her parents' place. Send me the proof – I'll kill her if anything happens to Mia, I'll fucking kill her."

The beeps speed up again. They seem louder this time.

"She did what? Why would she Google that? How could she be so psycho? I could seriously kill her. Call the police Tobias, give them everything you have, tell them everything you know! They better get to her before she does anything else. More importantly, they better get to her before I do, because if I find her first, I'll kill her! Elle cannot drug Mia and fucking get away with it! Don't tell me to calm down Tobias! I nearly lost everything I live for!"

Elle? My brain starts to remember. I was in the kitchen; I had some water and then everything went dark. And Elle did it? She hated me that much she wanted to physically harm me? My heart thumps up and down against my chest.

The beeps become ridiculously fast and I hear a nurse come rushing in.

"What's happening?"

"She's okay, just her pulse has gone higher than we would like, and her blood pressure is climbing again. She's stressed."

"What does that mean?"

"It means the baby will begin to stress too."

"Why is this happening?" Jacob's voice sounds scratchy and desperate.
Almost as if he is begging for something positive from the nurse.

"I think she has heard you Mr Jackson. I think she could hear you talking. I need you to help her now, keep her calm, for the baby's sake."

The nurse adjusts something in my hand, maybe a cannular, but I'm still not with it enough to be sure. I hear a little more noise, a pen scratching gently against some paper, a few taps of a machine maybe and then I hear her shuffle out of the door.

Jacob's hand grips mine.

"Baby, if you can hear me, I'm so sorry. You were right all along, it was Elle. I know you heard that call and that is not how I wanted you to find out but please know you are safe now. Nothing more is going to happen to you, to us."

I desperately want to open my eyes, but they feel stuck down. I feel like I'm floating around some dark wall-less open space. I want to feel in the room with Jacob so bad, but I can't get to him.

"They said the baby is fine..." he continues, uncertain. I know he is scared of what to say. He pauses and stutters several times, trying desperately hard to say all the right things.

"They found a strong muscle relaxer and a sleeping tablet in your system. But they said you will be okay. They said I found you just in time. I found you in the pool. You could have drowned, Mia, and honestly, if you had, I don't know what I would have..." He cuts off, composing himself, but I hear the shakiness in his voice, and I somehow know he has tears appearing in his beautiful brown eyes. "I heard you call out to me. At first, I thought I was dreaming, and I nearly went back to sleep, but somehow, I knew something was off. I realised you weren't beside me and that's when I knew. Somebody must have been looking over you that night, sweetheart."

His hand lightly drops onto my tummy.

"Somebody was looking over both of you, I should say."

My finger flickers against the palm of his hand.

"Mia! Baby, do it again if you can."

I'm not sure if the first one was a fluke, so I try, I concentrate hard, I try to bring myself back from floating and into my own body. I put all my energy into my finger and pray that I can push it up again but no luck. It's breaking me to know I can't communicate with Jacob. I know he needs me.

"Okay..." His soft whisper penetrates my ear. "Whenever you're ready then."

I feel a weight lower gently onto my ribcage and I imagine Jacob's head resting there, his deep brown hair flopped over, his pouting lips, his dark brown eyes staring at my tummy, waiting, praying, hoping.

I'm not sure how much time goes by, but the ward sounds noisier, so I think it must be morning by now. Jacob's head hasn't moved an inch.

I feel his finger drawing over my tummy, little shapes, circles, squares and then a heart.

"Daddy's here," he says so quietly it's almost inaudible. "You're going to be so lucky. You're going to have the best mum in the world. Let me tell you a little bit about Mia Johnson. She's a bad-ass sports journalist, she can even make bowls sound thrilling. She's an emotional person which means her feelings can be intense, but that's a good thing, see – when she loves, she loves with everything she has, and her love is so infectious. It makes you want to be around her *all* the time – and we're lucky because we actually will be. We'll be an awesome little family. Oh, and if you ever see your mum drinking red wine and talking to stray cats or swearing at hoovers, don't worry, she's not crazy – I don't think."

"Oi," I force through my thick dry throat. I feel like that weird zombie guy in *Hocus Pocus* who comes back from the dead and finally frees his sewn-up mouth for the first time in three hundred years.

Jacob's eyes have that glint back the second his eyes meet mine. Finally, I can see his face again.

"The baby's okay!" he blurts out, quick to reassure me, the relief obvious in his eyes.

I nod and clear my throat to try and speak again. "I know," I manage.

We both smile in unison. He looks so happy and relieved I think he could actually fist punch the air, but obviously he's too cool for a corny display like that.

"Elle has been arrested. Tobias texted me about an hour ago. It was her all along, but it's over now. Everything will be okay. You can breathe, Mia."

I'm so relieved; I nod gratefully and a small tear drips from the corner of my eye and down to my ear. Jacob's thumb rubs it away, but when I look up, his eyes are red and swollen too. He wants to cry with relief, but he holds back as best he can.

He leans down to place a kiss onto my mouth and I feel a tear fall from his eyes onto my cheek.

"Happy tears?" I quiz and he nods.

We are a right pair, both of us with quivering bottom lips and damp eyes, a mixture of relief and fear of what could have been weighing on our emotions. We both seem to come to the same conclusion – that we are both so grateful for the other.

Jacob leans in for another kiss.

"From now on, we drink from the tap," he laughs into my mouth before following up with another wonderful kiss.

"I love you, Mia Johnson."

"I love you too."

Printed in Great Britain
by Amazon

76017651R00113